"I guess being friends is safer..." David said as he framed her face with his hands.

Slowly he bent toward her. His lips settled over hers, his fingers slipping through her hair.

When they parted, he kept her close. "This doesn't feel like friends."

"No," she whispered, her voice barely working. That was what scared her. She'd been lousy at relationships in the past, and she wasn't going to put her son through that again. Pushing back, she moved to the side to put some space between them.

"I'd better go," he said and made his way to the door.

Lisa hurried after him, but he was gone. She'd tell him how she felt tomorrow. The hard part would be figuring out between now and then exactly how that was.

Books by Margaret Daley

Love Inspired

The Power of Love
Family for Keeps
Sadie's Hero
The Courage to Dream
What the Heart Knows
A Family for Tory
*Gold in the Fire
*A Mother for Cindy
*Light in the Storm
The Cinderella Plan
*When Dreams Come True
*Tidings of Joy
**Once Upon a Family
**Heart of the Family
**Family Ever After
**Second Chance Family
**Together for the Holidays

Love Inspired Suspense

Hearts on the Line
Heart of the Amazon
So Dark the Night
Vanished
Buried Secrets
Don't Look Back
Forsaken Canyon
What Sarah Saw
Poisoned Secrets

*The Ladies of Sweetwater Lake
**Fostered by Love

MARGARET DALEY

feels she has been blessed. She has been married more than thirty years to her husband, Mike, whom she met in college. He is a terrific support and her best friend. They have one son, Shaun.

Margaret has been writing for many years and loves to tell a story. When she was a little girl, she would play with her dolls and make up stories about their lives. Now she writes these stories down. She especially enjoys weaving stories about families and how faith in God can sustain a person when things get tough. When she isn't writing, she is fortunate to be a teacher for students with special needs. Margaret has taught for over twenty years and loves working with her students. She has also been a Special Olympics coach and participated in many sports with her students.

Together for the Holidays
Margaret Daley

Steeple
Hill®

Published by Steeple Hill Books™

STEEPLE HILL BOOKS

Steeple
Hill®

Recycling programs
for this product may
not exist in your area.

ISBN-13: 978-0-373-87559-7

TOGETHER FOR THE HOLIDAYS

Copyright © 2009 by Margaret Daley

www.SteepleHill.com

Printed in U.S.A.

The Lord is gracious, and full of compassion;
slow to anger, and of great mercy.
—*Psalms* 145:8

To Cyndee Cornell, a school district drug counselor
who gave me invaluable information
and inspiration.

Chapter One

A cross the large parking lot, Lisa Morgan spied her son in the center of a group of four middle schoolers at the side of the gymnasium, a pool of light illuminating the dark surrounding Andy. Fear lined her twelve-year-old's face as he straightened his shoulders, thrust out his chest and held his arms stiff at his sides.

Lisa increased her pace to a jog. She didn't want to over-react or her son would be upset that she embarrassed him. But something was wrong.

Joey, a child who had gone to school with her son for several years, grabbed Andy's arm. He wrenched free and started for the front of the gym. Another boy, on Andy's basketball team, blocked his escape. Suddenly Joey and three teammates closed in on her son, fists flying while one kid pinned Andy's arms against him.

Heart pounding, Lisa screamed for them to stop in the midst of the shouting that erupted from the boys who attacked Andy and threw him to the ground. She flat-out ran toward them.

From the front of the building a tall man dressed in warm-ups saw her then glanced to the side. Nearer to the scuffle, he shot forward, snatching one boy off Andy while saying, "Joey, Tyler, Brent, Sam, knock it off."

The kid who'd held her son down on the ground fled past her. She wanted to grab the adolescent and force him to stay, but her son needed her.

Only five more yards.

The sight of blood streaming down Andy's face twisted her stomach. Nausea rose rapidly. Swallowing the sickening sensation, she came to a halt near the man who had managed to pry the three boys from Andy.

"You all stand over there." He told the remaining boys and pointed to a spot near the double doors into the gym. "And don't move."

The forcefulness in his voice brought shivers to Lisa as she knelt to examine Andy's injuries—a cut lip, a bleeding nose. Although anger hardened his features, tears glistened in his eyes. The sight broke her heart. Andy had always been the pacifist, not the warrior.

Her vision blurred as she took out a tissue to wipe the blood from his face. "Are you hurt?"

Andy knuckled the moisture away and sat up. "I'm fine, Mom. Just a little disagreement." He averted his gaze and pressed his lips together.

"Just a little disagreement?" Lisa frowned at the lie that had come from her son. "I thought I'd taught you better than that. What's going on?"

Andy remained silent, staring at the ground.

Lord, doesn't he know by now that I won't let him down again? I made a promise to him. I won't break it.

"Andrew Morgan, I need an answer. Your shirt is torn, your lip is swelling as we speak, your nose might be broken and you might have a black eye if the redness is any indication."

While keeping track of the three boys by the gym doors, the tall man squatted next to Lisa. "What happened here, Andy?"

Lisa had been grateful the stranger had intervened as quickly as he had, but she would handle her family's problems. It was her responsibility and she wouldn't shirk that again. "I can take care of this. Thanks for helping." She turned back to her son, waiting for some kind of explanation.

"Nothing's going on," Andy muttered, scrambled to his feet and scurried back from her.

She started to rise when a hand on her arm stopped her. She went rigid at the touch and flinched away. Swinging her gaze to the stranger, she drew in a calming breath to keep from lashing out at the man. He'd only been trying to help.

"Let me see what I can find out," the stranger said.

"That's okay. I'll take care of it." Her voice held an edge of anger, not really directed at the man but the boys who had hurt her son.

His hand fell away, and she hurriedly pushed to her feet, rounding on the man who had also risen. He moved to the side to block her view of the three assailants. She needed answers from them, and the stranger purposely stood between her and the boys who had attacked her son.

"And just who are you?" She glared at the man who had to be over six and a half feet tall. His muscular arms and trim body spoke of someone who worked out and stayed in shape. No wonder he had easily plucked the three boys off Andy.

"I'm the new assistant basketball coach, David Russell. And you must be Andy's mother." He offered his hand to shake.

She ignored him and stepped to the side, needing some answers only the boys could supply.

He mimicked her move. "I felt some tension earlier while the team was practicing. That's why I followed them from the gym."

"I protect my own." She could remember suffering several beatings because she wouldn't let anyone hurt her son until the day Andy had stepped between her and her boyfriend's fist. Now it was her turn to do the same, and this take-charge man wasn't going to stand in her way of finding out why those boys attacked her child.

"I respect that, Mrs. Morgan, but they'll clam up if you charge at them with all the accusations I see on your face."

"Ms. Morgan," she said because that was all she could think to say in the wake of his words.

"Let me see what I can discover. Go ahead and take Andy home."

She opened her mouth to tell the man no, but the distress in her son's eyes, the blood still coursing down his face silenced her words. "Can I take Andy into the gym and have him wash up first?"

"Sure."

She approached her son. "Let's go inside and get you cleaned up. Your coach is gonna talk to the boys."

"Mom, don't let him arrest them." Andy clutched her arm, a frantic ring to his words.

"Arrest them?" Lisa slanted a look toward Mr. Russell who had the three lined up near the door while he spoke to them in a voice too low for her to hear anything. The expressions on the boys' faces ranged from insolent to angry to fearful.

"He's a cop."

"He is?" For just a second the urge to run swamped her. *No! I'm not that person anymore. I have nothing to hide. The Lord is on my side.*

"Yeah," Andy mumbled.

The stern look on the man's face demanded the kids' full attention, which he got. "He isn't gonna arrest them. He wants to know why they jumped you." She swung her gaze back to her son. "And so do I."

Andy narrowed his eyes on her. "I can take care of this. Leave it alone, Mom."

She clasped his upper arms, her heart breaking anew at the bloody sight of him. Definitely a black eye. "It's okay to ask for help."

He wrenched from her hold. "Not from my mother." Stomping toward the gym, he kept his focus straight ahead, never once glancing toward his three teammates and Mr. Russell.

Not from my mother. The words echoed through her mind, underscoring the quickly deteriorating relationship she and Andy had lately—ever since he'd started middle school this year. A band about her chest constricted her breathing. She fought for control and to keep her composure.

With a deep sigh, Lisa followed him into the building and waited outside the boys' restroom. Her willpower stretched to its limit, she managed to remain in the lobby instead of marching into the bathroom to help Andy clean up. Leaning back against the wall, she folded her arms over her chest and tried to calm her frazzled nerves after the long day at work and now this. Her son was in trouble, and he was pushing her away. Before the start of school, she and Andy had been close, but that was all changing and she didn't know how to stop it.

Mr. Russell entered the foyer of the gym and locked his gaze with hers. He strode toward her. The hard chiseled planes of his face formed a scowl and a muscle in his jaw line twitched. Even the crystalline blue of his eyes had darkened to a storm.

"How's Andy?"

"He's cleaning up." She jerked her thumb toward the restroom. "What did they say?"

"Not much. But I'll keep trying to find out."

"Why was practice over early?" If she had been a few minutes earlier, she could have prevented the fight—even if she'd had to throw herself bodily between Andy and the other boys. No one was going to hurt her son ever again.

"Coach Parsons had to leave. He let them go after they ran some laps. This was only my second practice. I'll make sure that doesn't happen again."

She pushed off the wall. "But we don't really know what happened other than some boys jumped my child. You said there was something going on during practice. What?"

"More whispering and jostling than usual. A few glares exchanged."

The door to the restroom opened, and Andy slinked out into the foyer. He kept his gaze averted, hanging his head.

"Andy," Coach Russell planted himself in front of the boy so he couldn't escape, "We can't help you if you don't tell us what's going on."

His usage of the word *we* surprised Lisa. She should protest the man's interference, but if Andy would tell him, she would welcome that. Now that she was thinking more calmly, she realized her initial reaction to the man had been wrong, had stemmed from her desire to make sure she met all her son's needs.

"It's nothing. I stepped on Joey's foot in practice when we both jumped up for the ball. He got angry. That's all." Andy never lifted his head but stared at the floor near his feet.

The coach snagged her attention, and she saw the doubt in his gaze. Her son was lying.

The man shook his head, massaging his nape. "I can help you if you let me. When you're ready to tell me what's really going on, I'll listen."

Andy trudged toward the exit and stopped at the double doors, but he didn't look back.

Disappointment glinted in Mr. Russell's blue eyes. "I figured he wouldn't say anything, but I was hoping he might." He shifted toward her. "I'll keep on top of this now that I know something is going on, Ms. Morgan."

"Lisa, please. Even at my job coworkers use my first name."

He again extended his hand to her. "David."

She fit her hand in his, not surprised by the firm clasp. "I'm sorry about the earlier response to your assistance."

He shrugged. "Not something I haven't encountered before. In the heat of a situation people often let intense emotions color how they response to even someone trying to help."

"I understand you're a police officer." Wariness laced her voice. Although she tried to mask her automatic response to anyone connected to the police, she could tell she hadn't succeeded by the look that flared into his gaze. She'd work on that because her problems years ago weren't because of the police.

"Yeah, twelve years on the force."

"Here in Cimarron City?"

"No, Dallas until I transferred here three months ago."

The sound of the door opening drew Lisa's attention toward the exit. Andy headed outside. "I'd better go in case one of the boys is still hanging around."

"I waited until they all got into their parents' car before coming inside."

She started across the lobby. "There was one who ran away."

"True, and I'll speak with Sam tomorrow. Good night, Ms.— Lisa."

The November night surrounded her in a chilling darkness when she left the gym. She called to her son to wait, but he kept walking toward her white Chevy. She jogged toward the parking lot and arrived as Andy slipped into the car's front seat.

Lord, I'm gonna need lots of patience. I don't understand what's going on with my son. I want my upbeat child back.

Lisa settled herself behind the steering wheel, started to switch the vehicle on but halted in mid-motion. Angling toward him, she fixed her gaze on him and tried to read his expression in the dim light from the security lamp as she said, "It's just you and me now. What's going on? Are those boys bullying you? I've heard some of the teens I work with talk about bullies at school."

Andy scrunched his mouth into a tight line. "I make good grades and Joey doesn't. It's really nothing. He'll move on to someone else soon. He gets bored easily."

"Bored! Andy, I'll talk with the principal. He can do something about Joey if he's bothering you at school."

He rounded on her. "Don't you dare! This is between me and Joey. If you step in, it will be ten times worse."

"But what if—"

"Mom, I made a hundred on a test today, and he didn't pass. The class laughed at him. He took it out on me."

"What's the other three guys' reason for participating?"

Andy shrugged. "Those are Joey's only friends, if you call them even that."

"Why didn't you say anything to Coach about this?"

"He's a cop. I don't want him stepping in. I don't trust the police. They'll say whatever they have to to trip someone up."

"Andy? Where's that attitude coming from?"

"You know." He folded his arms over his chest and stared straight ahead, the jut of his lower jaw accentuating his view. "I don't see how you can trust them either. They were the ones responsible for taking me away from you when I was eight."

"Honey, it wasn't that simple. I'd done some things—"

"Let's go home. I have a lot of homework."

Andy never wanted to talk about the past. Every time she tried to, he'd change the subject, which only made her feel worse. She had so much to make up for. "I think we need to talk about your feelings—"

"Mom, I'm tired and I want to change out of this bloody shirt." He gestured at the white T-shirt he wore under his jacket.

Splotches of red blemished the snowy color. A memory popped into her mind of another time when she'd been staring down at her own shirt and seen the same thing. She shuddered, shoving the past away. Maybe her son had the right idea—if you didn't think or talk about what happened four years ago—for that matter before that—it didn't exist. If only it were that easy.

Finally Lisa turned the key in the ignition, still stunned by her son's feelings regarding the police. When he wasn't so angry, she would try to discuss again what had happened four years ago when he'd been put into foster care and had lived at Stone's Refuge, a place where foster children stayed when there weren't enough people to take them into their homes. It had been no one's fault but hers. Taking drugs had made her dependent on a man who'd abused her and had tried to do the same with Andy.

That will never happen again. But the damage to her and Andy had been done, and she couldn't forgive herself for that.

Exhausted after a long shift and then attending the basketball practice, David pulled into the driveway of his sister's house and took a moment to compose himself before making his way to the porch. Blazing lights from almost every room greeted him as he approached. His sister was trying to get her two children more environmentally aware, but it didn't look like it was working.

Before David used the house key his sister had given him,

Max slammed open the front door. "Uncle David, you were supposed to be here half an hour ago. I'm starved and Mom said we couldn't eat until you came."

"Well, I'm here now." Stepping inside, David ruffled his eight-year-old nephew's hair. "What are we having?"

"Lasagna."

"Ah, my favorite." David drew in a deep breath of the spice-and meat-scented air. Something else teased his sense of smell, too. "And she baked some garlic bread."

"Yeah." His nephew smiled, revealing a missing tooth. Grabbing David's hand, he tugged him toward the kitchen. "Mom, Uncle David is *finally* here. Let's eat," the boy shouted in the hallway.

When David entered the room, Kelli McKinney put the casserole dish on one of the stove burners, then removed a foiled-wrapped loaf of bread. "Good thing I'm used to your tardiness," his sister said as she shut the oven door. "If I hadn't factored it in, we would have been eating a cold dinner or my children and I would have finished our meal ten minutes ago. Knowing Max's appetite, you would have been left with nothing to eat tonight."

David flashed a grin. "But you do know me. Thanks for waiting. It's been a long day and I'm about as starved as Max."

The boy plopped into a chair at the kitchen table.

"First, go get your sister and make sure your hands are washed." Kelli placed the lasagna on a trivet in the center of the four place mats.

"Ah, Mom, they're clean. I washed them…" His voice trailed off into silence as he glanced down at his fingers, splayed wide, and frowned. "I'll be back." Hopping up, he raced from the room.

David strode to the sink and washed his hands. "I don't want to set a bad example for your children."

"Never. I don't think you can do anything wrong in my son's eyes, or for that matter my daughter's." Kelli set the bread on the table, then removed the pitcher of tea from the refrigerator.

Do anything wrong? If only that were true. Then maybe he wouldn't be haunted by his memories.

"I don't know what I would have done if you hadn't come to Cimarron City when you did. Max was floundering after his father's death. He laughs and smiles now. That's because of your presence in his life."

But was helping his sister enough to atone for his past? He wished it was, but the emptiness he felt was spreading like a slow, festering disease bent on destroying him. "He's a good kid. He would have worked it out."

Kelli's mouth firmed into a stern look. "Don't sell yourself short. At least I don't have to worry about Max. Now if only I could say that about my daughter."

"Abbey was daddy's little girl. It's been only a year. Give her time." David settled his hands on his sister's shoulders, kneading the tension beneath his palms.

"She'll probably need at least five or six more years until she outgrows being a teenager. That's definitely part of the problem."

"Sit. I'll pour the tea." David took the pitcher and moved around the table filling each glass. "I'm proud of you, Kelli. You've done such a good job with what life has dealt you." *Myself, I'm not so sure about.*

"I didn't have a choice. I couldn't fall apart when Max and Abbey depend on me."

David pictured another mother struggling to raise an uncooperative child. Lisa Morgan had been fierce when she'd confronted him earlier. It reminded him of a she bear protecting her cub. A lot like his sister when it came to her children.

"You've got two amazing kids. Thirteen is a tough age, but Abbey will make it through."

"Well, while we're handing out compliments, you've been a great surrogate dad."

Which is the closest I'll come to having children. There was no way he would father a child in the world he lived. He set the pitcher on the table near him and sat as his niece and nephew charged into the room.

Abbey stopped in the middle of the kitchen, her hand going to her waist. "Mom, tell Max to be quiet. He thinks he knows *everything.* He's just a baby."

"No, I'm not!" His nephew squared off with his sister, his arms taut at his sides.

The "I want to hit you" look on Max's face immediately reminded David again of what had happened at the gym earlier with Andy Morgan. The thought of the scene when he'd followed the boys outside tightened his gut. A warning sign he'd learned to listen to. His niece went to the same school. Maybe he could find out what was really going on through Abbey because he didn't think the story that Andy gave his mother at the gym was the truth.

"Max. Abbey. Sit now." Kelli sent both of them a pointed look that brooked no argument.

After his sister said grace, which David went through the motions of participating in because of the children, Max snatched up the serving spoon and filled most of his plate with the lasagna. He ignored his sister to his right and instead gave the utensil to his mother. Abbey glared at her brother.

Before another skirmish erupted in the kitchen, David tore off a piece of the warm bread and then passed it to Abbey. Its aroma made his mouth water. "I started coaching this week. Today was my second practice. I think the team has a good chance of having a winning season. Maybe you know some of the boys playing on the team." He rattled off the names of several of them, ending with, "And our best players are Joey Blackburn and Andy Morgan. Do you know any of them?"

"The sixth graders?" Abbey wrinkled her forehead and nose as though the very thought of her associating with someone in the grade below hers was ridiculous.

"Any of them. The team has twelve- and thirteen-year-olds. Anything you tell me might help me when I'm working with them." David forked some of the tasty dish and brought it to his mouth.

"Well, Pierce is a dork, Michael is okay and Joey is a juvenile delinquent. What else do you want to know?"

David swallowed the mouthful of lasagna. "Why do you say Joey is a juvenile delinquent?"

"Because he'll do anything to make money. He's always scheming. He was in my grade and was held back two years ago. He hates school and makes sure everyone knows it, especially the teachers he has."

"Do you know Andy Morgan? He shows a lot of promise as a basketball player."

"Not much." Abbey shrugged. "We don't have any classes together. He's a sixth grader."

As though that was a disease. Ah, to be young and naive again. David took a bite of his still-warm bread and chewed it slowly. He hadn't learned too much more than he already knew from watching the boys the day before and today at practice. Except that Joey might be up to no good. Which made him wonder why was he on the basketball team? What did he have to gain, especially financially? And what was really going on with Andy and Joey?

He hadn't wanted his job as a police officer to interfere with coaching, but he would have to keep an eye on Joey and Andy. He knew from experience that their ages meant nothing when it came to committing a crime.

Chapter Two

On the floor, watching the twelve players going through a shooting exercise, David detected Lisa Morgan slipping into the gym. He glanced at his watch. She was early, but that didn't surprise him after what happened the day before. Good, she wasn't taking any chances there would be a repeat of yesterday's fight. He was relieved to see one parent who was conscientious because the tension between Joey and Andy was palpable.

Blowing the whistle, he signaled for the boys to circle around him. "I have an announcement to make. Some of you wanted to know where Coach Parson was. He's sick and will be out for a couple of weeks. He should be back by the first game. I assured him we would be ready to play the Spartans. What do you all say?"

A group cheer answered his question.

"I told him he had nothing to worry about. Are you gonna make a liar out of me?"

"No, Coach," the twelve boys shouted in unison.

"Okay, five laps around the gym before you leave, and I'll see you tomorrow at the same time."

As the players set out in a jog, David strode toward Lisa. She greeted him with a smile, making brief eye contact before her attention returned to the boys running in a tight group. David slid onto the bleachers next to her and followed the teammates completing their laps.

"Did you find out anything else last night from Andy?" he asked while his gaze took in her son slowing his pace slightly so he was at the back of the pack. David tensed when Joey threw a glance over his shoulder at Andy.

"Yes, this is because my son is a good student. Apparently Joey didn't like the fact that Andy made a perfect score on a test yesterday."

"Ah, so it wasn't the fact Andy stepped on Joey's foot accidentally in practice?"

She sent him a quick look. "It probably was both things."

Yeah, right. He didn't think it was either of those reasons. The practice today had only confirmed that in his mind. "I'm not so sure it is."

Lisa tensed. "Do all cops think everyone is lying?"

The accusation threw him off balance for a minute—not because he hadn't heard similar ones in the past, but because he hadn't expected it in this circumstance. "Truthfully we have to be wary of everyone. It helps keep us and others alive."

"That's sad."

Again a surprise. "Sad?"

"It's just such a cynical outlook on life. You always think the worse of someone."

In his career he'd been disappointed more than once at something a person had kept hidden from him. Now he didn't expect the whole truth from others. "I call it a realistic outlook, one that has kept me alive. People have things to hide. I think your son's hiding something."

She frowned. The boys finished their laps. Jerking to her feet, she started toward her son, paused and turned back. "I hope you can leave your job at the door when you come here to coach."

He rose slowly, suddenly tired. "I can never totally leave my job, as you say, at the door. I knew of one cop who didn't have his gun with him when he was off duty and ended up killed in a store robbery gone bad. Our job is 24/7."

She walked back the few feet that separated them. "My son is a good kid."

As the day before, her fierce attitude in Andy's defense surfaced quickly. He again saw some similarities between his sister and Lisa. *Is that why I want to help her?* "I never said he wasn't. But Andy doesn't want to tell you what's really going on between him and Joey. I would be asking myself why. That usually means something you don't want to hear, something not good."

The intensity in David's voice snaked about her, riveting her to the spot, holding her trapped. "I'm not sure he's hiding anything." *Andy doesn't lie to me. But then, in the past few months, he's changed.* Doubt nibbled at her confidence.

"But what if he is? Can you afford not to pursue it?"

She straightened her shoulders and tilted up her chin. "I'll keep an eye on him. Now if you'll excuse me, we have somewhere we need to go." She might have to spend some time around the new coach because Andy had told her last night he wanted to stay on the team, but that didn't mean she had to be the man's friend. They came from different worlds—their perspective on life polar opposites.

Andy raced toward her with his backpack. "Ready. I told Peter I would help him with the horses."

"You like to ride?" David removed the chain with the whistle on it from around his neck.

Her son's face lit up. "Yes. I do every week." He looked

down at his backpack. "I forgot my shoes. Be right back in a sec, then we need to get going."

"What stable?" Running his hand through his short black hair, David watched Andy run back across the gym to where the boys left their belongings while they practiced.

"It's not a riding stable. We help out at Stone's Refuge. There are horses for the children who are in foster care at the refuge. Peter Stone has a large barn with a lot of animals that have been abandoned. His collection keeps growing. He's thinking of building another barn strictly for the horses."

"My sister has told me a little about Stone's Refuge. There are five cottages with children in the state's custody? I think she said they recently expanded to include one cottage devoted to working with the more challenging teens with anger and addiction issues."

"Yes. They usually have around forty children at the refuge with seven at present in the Seven Steps to Healing Program in the fifth cottage. Does your sister volunteer there?" Lisa glimpsed a teammate—thankfully not one of the four who'd ganged up on Andy yesterday—saying something to him. He frowned and shook his head.

"I don't know if she has much time other than her family and the shelter."

"Shelter? Which one?"

"McKinney's Women Shelter."

"Who's your sister?" Lisa turned slightly to get a better view across the gym while Andy continued talking with the boy.

"Kelli McKinney."

"I know her. A good friend got me involved…" Joey came out of the boys' locker room and approached Andy and the other teammate.

"Is something going on?" David pivoted to look across the

gym at the kids who still lingered. "I'll take care of this." He started forward.

"Don't! Lisa grabbed his arm and halted his progress.

He stared at her with such potency that words fled her mind.

The warmth beneath her palm emphasized she still clasped him. She immediately dropped her hand and stepped back. "I promised my son I would let him take care of the problem as long as he thought he could."

"But—"

"Besides, Joey doesn't have the other three boys with him. He'll probably not do anything without them."

David glanced at her, one eyebrow raised. "What do you base that on?"

"A bully usually feels stronger when he has someone there to back him up."

"How do you know that?"

"Because I was bullied in middle school and high school by a girl who always had her clique there to back her up."

Why in the world had she shared something so personal about her life? But the truth was she hadn't thought of those girls in a long time, had determinedly refused to let them rule her life anymore. She'd been a young, impressionable teen-ager—before her life had totally fallen apart. But that was in the past.

Maybe the reason she'd let down her guard temporarily was because he'd revealed he was Kelli's brother. She and Kelli were friends. Lisa volunteered once a week at the shelter. She recalled Kelli talking about her brother moving to Cimarron City a few months ago and even mentioned him by his first name, but David was a common name. She had two Davids working for her at the restaurant.

The battle-ready tension that a few seconds ago had poured

off David faded to an interested alertness. He hung back next to her and followed the exchange between Joey and Andy. David's nearness sharpened her awareness of him. For a few seconds a connection zipped between them as they both watched the unfolding conversation of the two boys.

Andy's frown evolved into a scowl. He stepped away from Joey, but the bully moved to block him. Anxiety whipped down her length. She'd asked David not to interfere, but it was all she could do to stand here and do nothing. She slanted a look at the man next to her. A somber expression etched his features in stone.

When Andy glared and skirted around Joey, heading back across the gym, Lisa blew out a breath. "It's not easy respecting his wishes."

David faced her. "Sometimes you have to step in whether they want it or not. Don't hesitate if your gut tells you to."

Her glance strayed to his left hand. No wedding ring. That didn't really mean he hadn't been married at one time. "Do you have children?"

"No, just a niece and nephew, but as a cop I've seen a lot of things most haven't."

"Thanks for the advice. I'll take that under consideration."

He chuckled. "You don't sound too convinced."

"I'll work on that." When Andy moved toward the exit, Lisa hurried to catch up with him.

"What were you talking to Coach about?" her son asked in the lobby.

"You, of course."

Andy stopped right outside the gym. "Mom, I told you I could take care of it. I saw him talking to Joey before practice. Joey wasn't too happy about that."

"Is that what you and Joey were talking about?"

"No one likes to be called out by the coach." Andy spun on his heel and strode to the car in the parking lot.

Lisa followed him, turned the key in the ignition and pulled out into the light stream of traffic. "Andy, you really didn't answer my—"

"Mom, I'm fine. Can we please talk about something else?" He crossed his arms and stared out the side window.

"Okay. What do you think of Coach Russell?"

"He's a cop. What's there to say?"

"He had nothing to do with what happened four years ago. Besides, that officer was only doing his job, following up on the report from the hospital."

"Yeah, right. I told them you didn't hurt me. They didn't believe me."

She'd desperately needed help, and the state taking her son away from her had been the best thing that had happened to her. She'd gotten the assistance she'd needed. It had shaken the very foundation of her life and caused her to finally kick her drug habit. But like an alcoholic, she had to be constantly on the alert so that she would never slip back into old patterns. Thankfully the Lord was with her every step of the way, and she had a strong network of friends—two things she didn't have four years ago.

"I know I asked you last night, but I'm asking you again. Do you want to continue playing on the basketball team?"

His head turned away, Andy didn't answer for a long moment. "Yes. I love basketball. Joey is in most of my classes. Not being on the team won't help that situation."

"What will?"

"I'm sure you're right, and he'll get the point and move on," Andy said, but there was no conviction in his voice.

She hoped that would be the case, but she would be keeping

an eye on Joey and his friends, just as David had cautioned her to do. When it came to Andy she would do anything to protect him. At practice she was positive her son would be safe because of David, but what about all the other times? She never wanted to let Andy down again. She had once and nearly lost him for good.

When her car neared the front of the barn, Andy sat forward. "Mom, Roman's here. I hope nothing's wrong with one of the animals. "

"Maybe he stopped here first to see Peter before going home." Her son's agitation mounted. He would know Roman's patterns at the refuge because her son adored the man and wanted to be a veterinarian just like him when he grew up. When he'd been off for the summer, Andy had even interned with Roman once a week at his practice.

"Mom, he lives at one of the cottages. He only brings his van to the barn when he needs something from the back."

The last time an animal had died at the refuge Andy hadn't taken it well. She'd heard him crying in his room, but when she'd gone in to console him, he'd swiped away all evidence and pretended everything was okay. It hadn't been because for days he'd been so withdrawn that she'd decided to have a child psychologist, a good friend's husband, talk to him. She prayed it wasn't something serious.

The second Lisa turned off her Chevy, Andy leaped from the car and raced toward the barn. When Lisa entered a minute later, her fear something was wrong was confirmed. Her son had planted himself in the entrance into one of the stalls, worry imprinted on his face.

"What's wrong?" she asked when she came up beside Andy.

Inside Dr. Roman Devlin and Peter Stone, who had started the refuge years ago, hovered over an exhausted, wet foal lying near its mother on blood-covered hay. The mare's shallow, hard breathing sounded loud in the quiet, sending shivers of dread down Lisa. Sweat had dried white on the horse's neck, face and flanks.

Roman glanced toward Lisa, gesturing toward the mare. "She may not make it."

Her son paled. "Is the foal gonna be okay?"

"He is if I have anything to say about it." Roman returned his attention to the colt.

First Roman cleared the fluid from the newborn's nostrils, then he cut the cord and doctored the navel with an ointment while Peter moved to the mother. Kneeling beside her, he leaned close and spoke in soothing tones, stroking the mare's neck.

Lisa clasped her hands on her son's shoulders, the stiffness beneath her palms transmitting his tension. "Hon, I think we should leave and let them take care of everything."

"What if Roman or Peter need my help?" Andy asked, his voice thick with emotions. His lower lip trembled while he struggled not to shed the tears in his eyes.

Peter looked toward her son. "Andy, can you feed the goats and sheep for me? I was on my way to do that when she went into labor. You know where everything is."

Andy straightened. "Sure. Are there any other animals I need to see to?"

"Nope."

Andy hurried away.

"Thanks, Peter," Lisa whispered, her throat tight.

"When I saw the labor wasn't going well, I sent the other children back to the cottages. Thankfully Roman was there early and came to help, or I'm not sure the foal would have made it."

"It's a good thing I live close by for just such emergencies." Roman cleaned the foal's wet body.

Lisa stuffed her hands in her jacket pockets, the autumn air beginning to chill. "Is there anything I can do?"

"The labor was long and hard. She's old and worn out. You probably should keep Andy away just in case she dies. He used to ride Belle." Peter brushed his hand down the horse's neck.

"He'll give me a hard time about leaving, but you're right." Although Andy had his heart set on being a vet, she didn't know if he could take the death that came with the job.

The mare groaned. The sound brought Lisa's own tears to her eyes. Belle's body shuddered with each exhausted breath. The children at the refuge loved to ride the mare. Roman backed away from the colt and turned his attentions to Belle.

"Roman, what should I tell Andy?" Lisa asked as he gave the mare a shot.

"It's out of our hands. I'll know more in a few hours. If she makes it through the night, she should be all right."

Lisa's gaze swept to the foal struggling to get to its feet, determined to live. That same determination marked Lisa's life. She was going to make something of herself and prove to everyone she had been worth the second chance she'd been given all those years ago.

"Sorry I'm late. I had to drop Andy off at Stone's Refuge. He wants to help with the new foal. Belle had a hard labor and then her milk didn't come in." Lisa slid into the café booth where she met Whitney McCoy for their usual Saturday morning get-together.

A smile lit Whitney's eyes. "The kids were all talking about Belle and the colt when I went to the refuge yesterday. They've decided to have a little party today because Belle is alive and doing so much better now. A celebration of life, they're calling it."

"They are? I could use a celebration right now." The underlying tension at her house made Lisa want to scream in frustration. What was she doing wrong with her son?

"We should easily be finished by three. I'm going. You should come, too." Whitney took a sip of her coffee.

"You know, I think I will. It'll take my mind off…" She didn't want to think about her problems right now. They had kept her up all night, tossing and turning.

"That's twice you've alluded to something being wrong. I'm not letting the last one go." Whitney fixed her gaze on Lisa as though assessing what was wrong. "What's going on? Work? Andy?"

"When you see him today, you'll notice a black eye. Several boys jumped him after basketball practice. Andy won't say what's going on. How do you protect your child when he's not cooperating?"

Whitney leaned forward. "What happened with the boys who were fighting with Andy?"

"The coach talked to them and then their parents about what they did. And if anything else happens, they'll be removed from the team." Lisa fingered the menu she knew by heart. "I wanted to go to the principal, but Andy doesn't want me to do a thing. He says he'll take care of everything." Her son had always felt he should protect her and take care of things as though he was the man of the house. That hadn't changed over the years.

"Andy's a smart kid. Give him a chance, but keep an eye on him."

Lisa drew in a deep breath. "This is a case where I wish my child wasn't so independent. Anyway, I'd rather talk about something else."

Whitney waved her hand to get the waitress's attention. "We haven't ordered yet and I'm starved."

"Where's Kelli? I thought she was going to eat with us." Lisa asked, remembering the surprise when David had revealed he was her brother.

"She couldn't make it. She still needed to run to the store for some supplies for our project at the shelter." Whitney took the carafe of coffee and poured some more into her mug.

"I met Kelli's brother the other night." Lisa thought about their last encounter at the practice the day after the fight. The bond she'd felt with the man totally took her by surprise. Yes, he was concerned about her son, as she was, but there was more to it than that. She just couldn't pursue it—not with her background.

"Didn't she call him Dave or something like that? Other than that she hasn't said too much." Whitney dumped some more sugar into her coffee.

"His name is David Russell, and he's an officer for the Cimarron City Police Department. He's coaching Andy's basketball team." A picture of the man popped into Lisa's mind. Tall, commanding, handsome in a rugged way. And off limits.

"So is he single? Kelli never mentioned him having a wife or children."

"Yes. I didn't even realize who he was until he mentioned Kelli's name."

"So what do you think of him?" Whitney's probing gaze fastened onto Lisa.

"Interesting."

"Interesting how?"

"I see those wheels turning in your mind, Whitney McCoy." Lisa shook her head. "But you can quit thinking there's anything between us." Yes, one day she would love to find a good man, but with her past, that possibility certainly wouldn't include a police officer. But for the present, she didn't want a romantic relationship. She had so many other things to focus on, especially raising her son.

A waitress appeared at the booth with her pad and pen to take their orders.

Lisa quickly perused the breakfast dishes and decided on her usual.

Whitney laughed. "We aren't going to change our orders, are we? I've ordered the same thing ever since we started meeting here on Saturday. I didn't even change what I ate for breakfast when I was pregnant with Courtney, and believe me, I had some strange food preferences then."

"How's your adorable little girl?" Lisa took the hot water the waitress brought her and poured it into her mug, then dunked her tea bag into it.

"She went for her two-month checkup yesterday and is doing great." Whitney's face glowed with happiness.

Lisa wished she could have another child, one she could do right by from the very beginning, but that didn't appear to be in her future—at least not her immediate future. And truthfully she had all she could handle right now with Andy and the added responsibilities at work. But the image of David Russell lingered in her thoughts as Lisa enjoyed her breakfast.

Lisa stood in the center of one of the renovated rooms at the women's shelter. Over the years the place had grown from utilizing the first floor of a two-story building to recently expanding to the second floor when a tenant moved out, which would allow more women and their children to be served in the community. All of this had started with one woman's vision, dedicated to Kelli's sister-in-law who had died at the hands of her husband.

"I'm finally here," Kelli said as she rushed through the doorway with her arms loaded with supplies.

Behind Kelli, her brother entered, carrying a stepladder and a toolbox. His look immediately swept to Lisa. She dragged her gaze from his, focusing on her friend who ran the shelter. She had already thought too much about him today!

"If we can get the rooms painted today, the carpet can be laid Monday and the donated furniture moved in Tuesday—" Kelli smiled, placing the bags of supplies on the unfinished floor, "we'll be able to use them by Tuesday afternoon. I have families sharing rooms right now. As you know, they need some privacy. So much has been disturbed in these women's lives. This is so needed, and the Lord answered my prayers when the tenant left and this floor became available for our use."

"Where do you want us to start?" Lisa's neck tingled as though someone was staring at her. But she kept her attention on her friend who distributed the brushes and cans of paint, then directed the volunteers to their room.

"Lisa, you can work in the one next to this one. David, will help you." Kelli gave her the supplies needed, then turned to her brother. "David, you can leave the ladder and toolbox in here in case anyone needs them. I already have a stepladder next door."

Great. So much for not thinking about him. Without looking toward David, Lisa hurried from the room and into the one next door.

At a much more sedate pace, David came through the entrance with a brush and his own can. One corner of his mouth lifted in a grin, his eyes gleaming. "Nice to see you under different circumstances."

The last time she'd seen him had been at Thursday night's practice, but she'd made it a point to stay back. The whole practice she'd discovered his keen regard straying to her as though trying to delve into the secrets she kept hidden. Now she would be trapped in a fourteen-by-fourteen-foot room with him for a good part of the day.

"Which end?" he asked, his voice flat.

"I beg your pardon?"

"Your body language is screaming you want to keep your

distance so I figure you can take one end of the room and I'll take the other. That's about as far away as we can get in here." He gestured to the small enclosed space. "I suggest you take the end closest to the door in case you need to escape."

Her mouth dropped open. "I—I…" She glanced down at her rigid stance and forced herself to uncurl her hands at her sides. "I'm sorry."

Both of his eyebrows shot up. "Sorry, for what?"

"Isn't it obvious? I didn't mean for you…" She couldn't finish her sentence because she would be admitting she didn't want to have anything to do with him, that a man like him—a cynical police officer who had seen the bad side of the life she'd lived for years—made her feel uncomfortable, almost scared of the emotions he brought to the surface along with the memories. If only she could forget where she'd come from. But she knew she couldn't.

"Didn't mean to make it so obvious you don't want to be around me?"

"Yes," she finally said when she knew she couldn't avoid the truth.

"Why, Lisa? Does this have to do with your son and what I said to you or something else?"

Anger surged through her. "Ah, the suspicions. Do you have any peace always suspecting someone is up to no good?"

He frowned. "I didn't exactly say that."

"Yes, you did." She breathed deep inhalations to calm herself down. She wasn't going to spend the whole day riled up because of this man. "Yes, I was affected by what you said concerning Andy. You think he's lying. You think he's caught up in something bad. You think…" Her words spluttered to a stop as David advanced the few feet separating them, his glare drilling into her.

"I never said he was caught up in something bad. Is that what you think? That Andy is in some kind of trouble the police would be interested in?"

"No!" His nearness set her heart beating rapidly. She took a step back. "What I'm afraid of is that Andy is being bullied like I was. I don't want my son living in fear like that."

The intensity in David vanished. "Neither do I. I want to help him."

"Why?"

His eyebrows crunched together. "Now you're the one who sounds suspicious." He shook his head and moved back a few paces. "He's on the team I'm coaching. I think he's a good kid, and don't want to see him come to harm. I've seen what bullies can do, too. Are those enough reasons for you?"

Her anger deflated with each reason he gave her. Her son was leery of the police, and she realized she was, as well. *Old habits die hard.* For years while taking drugs she'd avoided police officers. Now she faced one who wanted to help her son. "I'm sorry." She quickly held up her palm to stop him saying anything. "And don't ask me why. I'm sorry because we've gotten off on the wrong foot. Can we start over?" She covered the space between them and held out her hand. "Hi, I'm Lisa Morgan, Andy's mother."

He shook her hand, his long fingers engulfing her much smaller ones. "I'm David Russell. It's nice to meet you." He grinned. "Where do you want to start painting?"

Still feeling the lingering warmth form his touch, she purposely pointed toward the end of the room away from the door. "Let's start there and work our way toward the escape route."

He chuckled. "I like that plan."

After opening the only window to allow fresh, cool air inside, she picked up her can and brush and took it to the far end while David grabbed his paint and some other supplies they would need. "I'm glad there isn't any carpet. The few times I've painted I'm not sure I improved the room when I was through. It spattered everywhere!"

"In that case, why don't you tape and I'll use the roller on the walls, then we can both go back and fill in with our brushes."

"Sounds like a game plan to me."

For the first thirty minutes Lisa worked in silence, but soon the quiet got to her. She began humming to break the silence.

"I'm gathering you like to talk while you work?" On the stepladder, David paused in rolling the wall and glanced down at her.

"And you don't?" Lisa asked from her position on the floor under the window where she was taping off the wood.

"I was a patrolman for years and worked alone, driving around in my car. I got used to the quiet."

"I work in a busy restaurant where there is constant noise. I'm used to that."

"Where do you work?"

"I manage one of The Ultimate Pizzeria Restaurants, the main one where there are games and a few rides." She stood and stretched. "Of course, adults have been known to do the go-carts, too."

"Sorta like an indoor theme park?"

"Yeah, a small one. Have you been there yet?"

"No, but my nephew is begging me to take him."

"You should bring him. It's a fun place for the whole family. This restaurant in the chain has a different feel from the others. Noah told me the other day he's adding the games and rides to the ones he has in Dallas, Tulsa and Oklahoma City. He wants to emphasize families having fun together." She grasped her can and brush so she could start filling in the gaps. "Did you ever go to the one in Dallas? That's where you lived before coming here, right?"

A scowl descended on his face. He turned back to working. Silence, like a high wall, filled every corner of the room.

Chapter Three

"Kelli said something about her brother coming to help her with the kids. Is that why you moved?" Lisa asked behind David, standing on the stepladder.

He tried to push away the image of a child, similar in age to Andy, who wouldn't leave his mind. But the boy's blank stare dominated David's thoughts. It taunted him, daring him to tell Lisa the real reason he'd left his home of sixteen years to come to Cimarron City. Because if he was truthful with himself, it wasn't because of his sister and her family, but the fact he couldn't stay another day in Dallas, a constant reminder of what had happened on the streets.

"Wait. You don't have to say anything. It's none of my business. I tend sometimes to get too chatty and want to know everything about a person right away."

His fingers about the roller ached from his tight grip. Like a strobe light, the picture of the thirteen-year-old flashed in and out of his mind as it had at odd moments for the past two years.

"David, I shouldn't have pried. I'm sorry. I just remembered Kelli saying once how hard it is to raise two children by herself.

She does so much for others. I was glad to hear she would get some help."

Lisa's words felt like they came from far away. In his thoughts the scent of blood mingled with the real odor of the paint. His chest tightened. *Dead. Because of me. How do I live with that?*

Fingers grazed his elbow. He blinked, slowly seeing the beige wall in front of him.

"David, are you all right?"

He drew oxygen into his lungs to ease the constriction about his upper torso, then heaved a deep sigh. "Yes." Again silence hung between them, and he realized he had to say something about Dallas. "I needed a change of scenery. When this detective job opened up in the town Kelli lived, I made the move. She never said anything to me, but from our conversations on the phone I could tell she needed help with the kids." Which was all true. But he hadn't told anyone, even his sister whom he was close to, the anguish he fought every day when he allowed himself to remember.

"How long have you've been a detective?" Lisa moved away from him, sitting again on the floor to paint the area above the baseboard.

After inhaling and exhaling several composing breaths, he said, "I made detective in Dallas about a year ago." He'd thought that changing jobs within the department would make his life bearable, that not having to put on his uniform every workday would wipe the child's face from his mind. It hadn't worked. Hence the move to Cimarron City. These last few months had been better until something forced him to think of the past.

"What area do you work in?"

"Robbery/Homicide."

"A few months back there was a robbery at the café down the street. The police chased him into one of the residential areas. He jumped a fence into a yard with a pit bull. He regretted that decision. When the officers arrived, the dog had him cornered in a tree, the bag of money he stole scattered all over the ground below. Thankfully some robbers make bad choices and get caught."

"I always hate foot pursuits." He tossed her a grin. "The shoes aren't what I would choose to run a race in."

"You look like a runner." Her gaze traveled down his length.

"I try to four or five times a week." This topic of conversation he could deal with.

"I half jog, half walk in the morning before I have to be at work. I'm trying to work up to jogging the whole time. I haven't made it."

"How long have you've been doing it?"

"A year."

He chuckled. "Sounds like someone's heart isn't in it."

"You could say I'm halfhearted."

"At least you're honest about it."

She caught his gaze. "I'm always honest. That's what the Lord expects us to be."

"I have a feeling God is looking down on the people of Earth and shaking His head in disappointment. I think He's forsaken us."

"I guess I shouldn't be surprised by your cynical attitude, but He hasn't forgotten us at all."

"How am I supposed to believe in God when I see so much suffering and injustice?"

She stared at the baseboard, her hand hovering over the can for a few seconds before dipping her brush into the paint. "So you don't think people can make mistakes and still believe?"

"Do I think someone who killed a person should be able to waltz right into heaven as though nothing happened? No."

*How's God, if there really is one, going to forgive me, even
though it was in the line of duty?*

"Some of the people Jesus gathered around him were im-
perfect, the lowlifes—prostitutes, a tax collector. God forgives
anyone who truly repents."

"A drug addict who sells her child to get money to buy dope?
A man who murders his family?" he asked in a harsh tone, not
able to stop the anger, more at himself, from deluging him.

Lisa winced. "Anyone can be saved. That doesn't mean
those people won't pay for their crimes against humanity. They
should, but the Lord will forgive them."

Frowning, he snorted and turned his focus on finishing the
wall he was painting. What a Pollyanna outlook! He didn't
believe there was a God like that. There had been a time he had.
It had taken him only a few years on the streets to see what
people would do to their "loved" ones to change his mind.

Standing next to Andy, Lisa couldn't believe that she was
on the other side of David at Stone's Refuge while Peter ad-
dressed the small crowd. He'd decided to use this time to celebrate all the new animals at the refuge. A child who was in
charge of taking care of the new pet led it in front of the other
children and adults amidst the clapping.

Andy and Gabe brought Belle and her colt for everyone to
see. The group roared and cheered. Andy grinned from ear to
ear. His heart was so full of love, especially for the abandoned
animals at the refuge, probably because at one time he'd feared
that she had abandoned him as she'd struggled to get off drugs.
Every day she tried to make up for that mistake. Most days she
felt good about what she had accomplished, but lately with
what was going on with Andy at school, she was beginning to
have doubts.

Earlier after David and she had finished helping to paint the additional rooms for the shelter, just about everyone had decided to attend the celebration. They were ready to party after working hard. Kelli persuaded David to come along and see the refuge for himself because he had mentioned being interested in it.

There was a time when they had discussed Dallas that a flash of pain had contorted his expression for a brief moment. That glimpse of vulnerability in his tough-guy armor pierced through the protective shield she had about her heart. She couldn't shake the feeling something happened to him in Dallas that he was running away from. If that were the case, she had firsthand experience that he could never run fast enough and far enough to escape the past. It would cling to him like a heavy, wet coat draped over his shoulders, dragging him down. Hopefully he would discover that and shed his coat.

When she was with him, she found herself wanting to help him, and yet all her common sense said to stay away from him. She couldn't forget what he'd said about the drug addict. His contempt was evident in his tone, and it stressed how impossible it would be for them to have any real relationship. Whoa! Relationship? Why was she even thinking along those lines?

Andy turned toward her. "Mom, do you think Belle is really all right?"

"Hon, quit worrying about her. Roman said she's fine now."

"He said I could help feed the foal whenever I'm here in the afternoon until Belle's milk comes in. We'll use a bottle."

"You have basketball practice four times a week after school. Will six-thirty be too late to help with the foal?" Behind her, she sensed David shift toward her when she mentioned basketball practice.

"If it isn't, can I come every night to feed him?" Andy's expression held a hopeful expectation she couldn't say no to.

"So long as you still get your homework done before going to bed."

"I'll go see." Her son hurried toward Roman, who stood by his wife, Cathy. The couple were talking with Hannah, the manager of Stone's Refuge. Her husband, Jacob, was on its board and one of the founding members. Hannah and Jacob had rescued her when she had been abandoned and had nowhere to live four years ago.

"I once had a baby squirrel that must have fallen out of its nest because I found it on the ground, stunned, by itself. I was so excited because I finally had a pet, my first one. I tried feeding it with a bottle," David said near her ear.

His warm breath on her neck sent chills down Lisa. Her heartbeat increased. She spun around and took a step back. "What happened to the squirrel?" The question came out in a breathless rush.

"It didn't make it. I was six and cried myself to sleep the night it died. I decided not to rescue any more animals after that. I didn't want a pet if it was going to hurt that much."

She pictured this large, muscular man who protected people for a living crying as a little boy over his first pet dying. Something inside her softened toward him and made her want to forget all the barriers between them. "Did you ever have another one?"

"We had a dog a few years later, but my parents got it at a pet store. At first I didn't want to have anything to do with it, but Buddy wouldn't stop pestering me, wanting me to play. Before long he went everywhere with me except school. And when he died it hurt worse than the squirrel, but I didn't regret one moment of knowing him." David swept his arm to indicate the barn and its surrounding area. "I like this setup and the fact that the only animals here are abandoned ones and their offspring. I wouldn't mind helping out at the refuge when I have the time."

His story produced a tightness in her throat. She swallowed hard. "Hannah is the one to talk to about that. Of course, Peter oversees the animals and barn. What were you thinking of doing?"

David rubbed his chin and stared off to the side for a moment, then fastened his gaze on hers. "I've been toying with this idea since I heard about a friend on the police force in Dallas doing it with some children from low-income housing. I'd like to teach a tae kwon do class to the children involved in this. It will help build their self-confidence."

"Hannah might go for that."

"And I want Andy to take it, too."

"Why?"

"If he's being bullied, it will help him feel he can take care of himself."

"Are you suggesting he use tae kwon do moves on Joey and his friends?"

David frowned. "No, but as I said, if Andy feels confident, it will come across when he's interacting with Joey and his friends. Bullies go after people they perceive as weak. Not the strong ones. I want Andy to come across as strong."

"I'll talk to him, but I'm not totally convinced it's the right choice for my son."

Andy skidded to a stop next to her. "Roman said it was okay if I came after six-thirty. Gabe is gonna do it in the morning before he goes to school."

"You know some evenings I have to go back to work after I pick you up from practice. I'm the manager now, so I have to make sure the jobs are covered and there's enough workers at the restaurant."

"Ah, Mom, this is important to me. Belle would want me to do this for her baby until she can."

"We'll see what we can work out."

Andy beamed. "Gabe and Roman are gonna show me what to do as soon as Roman walks Cathy back to the cottage. She's not feeling well."

As her son left to join a group of boys near the paddock, David asked, "Who's Gabe?"

"That's the kid on Andy's right. They are best friends. Gabe lived at the refuge in one of the cottages until Hannah and Jacob adopted him. Actually they've adopted several children who once lived in a cottage here. I think if they could they would adopt everyone who comes through the refuge, but some of the kids go back to their families."

"I don't understand sending a child back to a bad situation. As usual the courts are too lenient. I've seen some children who were put back with their parents only to be taken away again because the bad habits returned. In my experience, people don't usually change."

The feelings his presence generated in her caused Lisa to dream of having more, but his words reinforced the impossibility of that. Her life was so different than what it was four years ago because of the Lord's grace and mercy. She'd been heading for complete destruction and God saved her. Now she had hope she could raise her son to do the right thing and that she could make a difference in the world. "You really don't believe people change?"

"Basically, no. I haven't seen much evidence of it."

"Not everything is black or white. Life is full of shades of gray."

"Often those shades of gray are excuses we use to justify what we did."

"Why don't you talk with Hannah about the tae kwon do class?" She turned away to search for Hannah, to hide the sadness she felt creep into her expression. Her friend was showing her toddler a new litter of puppies in a pen just inside the barn. "There she is." Without waiting for David's reply, she started toward the Stone Refuge's manager.

How can David live a life with no hope? Has seeing so much darkness made him that way?

While Hannah's child played with a puppy, her friend rose as Lisa and David approached the pen. "Gabe said that Andy was going to help with the foal. He was so excited they would be the ones responsible for Belle's baby. Peter said Gabe and Andy could name the colt."

Somehow she would have to work out a way to get Andy to the ranch and back those evenings she had to work. "Knowing those two, they'll spend days trying to come up with the perfect name."

Hannah laughed. "You mean weeks. I remember the last animal they got to name." She looked toward David next to Lisa. "What do you think of our refuge?"

"What I've seen has been impressive."

"I'll have to give you a deluxe tour one day or better yet, Lisa, you can. You know the place as well as I do."

"Sure, anytime." *Why am I being constantly thrown together with him? What are You trying to tell me, Lord?*

"I have a proposal for you. I'd like to teach some of the children at the refuge tae kwon do. What do you think of me starting a class once or twice a week?" David asked.

"I like that. Now that we have the new recreational hall, there's a place for those kinds of classes. I've been looking at ways to expand what we have to offer because we have the space to do more. Let me talk to each couple who run the cottages and see who they have who would be interested in tae kwon do. Could you start next Saturday morning?"

"Sure. The basketball games we'll be playing soon are all on Friday evening or Saturday afternoon."

Hannah's eyes grew round. "Oh, no. Emily is trying to carry a puppy away." She hurried after her child who waddled toward the back door of the barn, the small animal cradled against her chest.

David chuckled. "That age keeps their parents on their toes."

"Not just that age. Every stage a child goes through has good and bad aspects. Although I'm not sure what the good points of teenagers are." Thinking back to her own teenage years, she could still recall the trials, so often hormone-driven.

"I know. My niece is so emotional. Everything is a big deal to her. I keep thinking she's gonna grow up to be an actress."

"Lately I've been seeing more mood swings in my son."

"Being married and having children isn't easy. I chose not to go that route because my job isn't easy on a family. I saw what some of my fellow officers went through with their marriages falling apart and decided not to go there."

If and when she ever became interested in a man again, she wanted marriage. David sounded dead set against it. "But you aren't them. Marriage requires a lot of work. Maybe they weren't willing to do that."

"Have you ever been married?" He pinned her with a questioning look.

Her lack of a husband wasn't a secret, and yet she hated to share it with a man who had seen so much of the bad side of life and believed the worst in people. She returned his steadfast gaze, realizing there wasn't any way to say it but straight out. "I've never been married. I was fifteen when I had Andy." She hoped her-matter-of fact tone would put an end to the discussion that she should never have opened.

"That must have been hard on you."

You can't even begin to realize how hard. She wanted to say those words to him, but she'd already revealed more of herself to David than most people except her close friends. Her association with Andy's father had started her downhill slide until she'd hit rock bottom four years ago. She would never put herself in that position again. The past four years she'd learned to stand on her own two feet and little by little had pulled herself up out of the gutter.

"Being a single mom isn't easy, but Andy is a good kid. He's made the job so much easier."

"But you're worried about him?"

"It's hard to be a mother and not worry about your child." At least for her. She doubted her mother had ever been concerned about her.

"Then I hope he's at my tae kwon do class next Saturday."

"We'll see."

Behind schedule, David parked in a space at the side of the gym and hurried around to the front. He wanted to be there when the first boy arrived. He didn't want there to be anymore trouble like what had happened last week with Andy. Seeing the concern and pain in Lisa's eyes that evening unsettled him. Although he never wanted to be a parent, he could image how awful it would be to watch someone beating up your child.

Rounding the corner, he glimpsed Lisa's Chevy in the parking lot already. In that moment, he realized he had been looking forward to seeing her again. He couldn't deny his interest. He saw her on the sidewalk in front of the gym with her son, an automatic smile came to his lips until he glimpsed her frown.

With a scowl, Andy dropped his backpack at his feet. "Mom, why can't you take me to the refuge this evening? I have to feed Tiger his bottle. He needs me." He closed the space between them and lowered his voice. "And you don't have to walk me to the door. What do you think the other guys will say?"

"I just want to see if you can leave practice a little early so I can take you home and get back to work. We are two people short. I need to be there for the dinner hour."

Andy pinched his mouth together in a tight line.

"I'll call Peter and tell him to get someone else just for today."

The urge to help, to see a smile on Lisa's face prodded David forward. He stopped a few feet from the pair. "I can take Andy to the refuge, then drop him at home or the restaurant, whichever you want."

Andy's gaze zeroed in on him while Lisa spun toward him. "You look tired. I can't ask you to do that."

After the long, exhausting day trying to piece together information and leads on a new robbery gang hitting houses and businesses, all he'd wanted to do was go home and work out to ease his stress. That would have to wait now. "You didn't. I offered. I have to go out to the refuge anyway this week to check out the recreation center. I thought I would also talk to a few kids and answer any questions they might have about the class. Tonight is as good a time as any. Andy, you could introduce me to some of the kids at the refuge."

The boy stiffened. "Sure." He bent over and snatched up his backpack, then marched up to the double doors into the gym and disappeared inside.

"Are you sure?"

"I'd like to get to know him better. Maybe I can figure out what's going on because it's affecting the team. If they're going to win any games, they need to work together. Andy is my best shooter on the team. Right now I have a division between Joey's group and the boys who are Andy's friends."

Doubt flitted in and out of her dark blue eyes. Finally resignation won. "Fine." Lisa hooked her short, white blond hair behind her ear, her movements jerky as though she were trying to hide her agitation but not succeeding. "If you're sure about going out to the ranch."

"I am. Have you decided if Andy can do the tae kwon do class?"

"I asked him. He told me he wasn't interested."

"Then give me a chance to talk him into taking the class. That is, if it's okay he learns tae kwon do. I still think it would make him feel more confident in himself."

"Fine and bring him by The Ultimate Pizzeria. He can have dinner there. I'm not sure how late I'll be at work tonight."

"You got it." David tipped an imaginary hat and started for the entrance into the gym, feeling like whistling after a difficult day on the job.

"Wait."

He turned, facing Lisa. "Yeah?"

"Thanks, I appreciate you taking Andy out to the refuge. I know you didn't have to. That you're helping me." Her generous mouth lifted slowly in a smile.

He grinned. "You're welcome."

He did whistle a catchy tune he'd heard on the radio on the way to practice. When he walked into the gym, he went into the storage room to retrieve the cart of basketballs. By the time he came back, the twelve boys had all arrived, each faction on different sides of the cavernous room. Determination to meld the players into a true team fueled him through the practice. He firmed his resolve to get to the bottom of what was happening between Joey and Andy, and his best chance, even with the hostile vibes he felt pouring off Andy, was with him.

An hour and a half later on the ride to Stone's Refuge, he began his campaign to win the boy over so he would open up about what was going on. "Who should I talk to about taking tae kwon do? Any suggestions?" David glanced toward Andy who kept his face turned, his gaze glued to the side window by him.

While the child shrugged, he curled his hands into fists. "I guess the older guys."

"How about your friend Gabe?"

"Maybe."

"How about you?" David asked while he waited at a stoplight.

Andy swung around and looked at him, his tense body screaming his angst. "I don't think Mom wants me to."

"She told me today you could if you want. There are exhibitions and tournaments where you can show off your skills. It teaches you discipline, to focus your mind."

"I like basketball." Andy uncurled his hands, but he still sat ramrod straight.

"It'll help you to be a better basketball player. It did for me. I played college ball, and when I began taking tae kwon do, my game improved a lot. I even had a chance to go to the pros, but I didn't want to."

"You didn't want to be a pro basketball player?"

The incredulous tone in the boy's question made David chuckle. "I know, but I wanted to make a difference. I'd wanted to be a police officer since I was ten." He'd become the police officer, but he didn't know about making a difference.

"Do you ever regret not being a pro player?" Some of the tension eased from Andy's shoulders.

There was a time he'd been naive enough to think he was doing some good, but now he knew better. The first time he was spat on, he shook it off. He was there to help. The people would see that. But after a while and he was still being spat on and called all kinds of names, he couldn't shake it off any longer. "No, I really didn't have the desire needed to be a successful player in the NBA."

"Well, I do. Then I can be rich enough to take care of Mom so she doesn't have to work so hard." Andy angled more toward him.

"She works all the time?" He'd had a hard time shaking her from his mind, to the point he went to bed thinking about her and woke up in the morning with her in his thoughts. He shouldn't have a thing to do with her because she was the marrying kind and was responsible for a kid. If he were sensible, he'd stay away from her in the future.

"Yes. She wants to buy a house one day for us. She's been saving, but things are always happening. Last month she needed a new tire because of a blowout that couldn't be fixed. When Jacob checked all her other tires, it ended up she needed all four. She'd been driving around on bald ones."

"Hannah Hartman's husband?"

"Yeah, he helps us when he can. Jacob's cool." Andy's face relaxed into a half grin.

"I've heard good things about him. He's the pediatrician for my sister's two kids." David pulled into the long drive at the ranch that led to the barn, its large structure in the distance announcing the conversation was about to come to an end. "Will you think about taking tae kwon do?"

"Why do you want me to?" Suspicion sounded in his question, the tension returning to the boy's face.

"When I saw you Saturday at the refuge, I noticed the kids look up to you. If you do, others will." David paused, trying to decide how to phrase the other reason. He always wanted to be truthful and up front with Andy. "And I think it will help you build confidence in yourself. If you try it and don't like it, you can always quit."

"I'll think about it."

David parked in front of the barn. "I'll come with you, then we can go over to the recreation center. Okay?"

"Sure." Andy hopped from the car and rushed toward the entrance.

David gripped the steering wheel and watched the boy almost flee from him. For a few minutes, Andy had relaxed while talking with him about basketball, then at the end his suspicion had leaked back into his voice. Andy didn't trust him. When Coach Parson had let it slip during the second practice he'd been assisting that he was a police detective, he'd noticed some of the boys' reactions. It didn't bother most, but Andy and Joey had tensed. Joey had even taken a step back. His own suspicion heightened. Why were the two boys wary of the police? Did they have something to hide?

Lisa gave change to the man who had ordered two large pizzas, then handed him his glasses to fill at the drink fountain. Nathan returned from taking his break.

"It's busy tonight," the young man said as he stepped in to run the cash register.

"How are your classes going at the university?" Lisa asked, scanning the restaurant to make sure everything was running smoothly.

"Hard, especially physics. I see the new employee is doing a good job."

"Yeah. Mitch seems like a good worker, so it would be nice to train him in the game room to fill in when someone's gone. That's the job he wanted. We just don't have any openings at the moment."

"This is the place to work," Nathan said, grinning at the new customer approaching. "I hear the owner's building another restaurant in Cimarron City and making the game room bigger to include even more rides like a go cart race track and a miniature golf course."

Lisa waited until the father of three rambunctious kids ordered and left before answering. "Yeah. I think it's a smart move, and I told him I hope I'll be considered for the manager position. I could see Andy living at a place like that. I'd have to drag him home. Noah's even talking about having an indoor basketball court. He wants it to be the place the kids come to play and hang out."

"The bad comes with the good."

Lisa chuckled. "My, you're getting cynical. You remind me of my son's basketball coach." As she spoke, she glimpsed the object of her statement and Andy entering The Ultimate Pizzeria and stepped from behind the counter as Andy strode toward her. "How did it go?"

"Tiger drank the whole bottle. Roman said he's a little chowhound."

"Go give Nathan your order." As her son moved to the counter, Lisa linked her gaze to David's. His intensity arrested the flow of her breathing. For a few seconds she forgot to fill her lungs. Finally she managed to inhale a deep breath and smile at David. "Thanks for bringing him here."

She started to turn away when he said, "I thought I would eat dinner, too. No reason to go home to my apartment and eat alone. Have you eaten yet?"

Before she could give David an answer, Andy came up to her frowning.

"Mom, do you know who that new guy is?" Andy gestured toward Mitch clearing off a table. "That's Joey's older brother." With an eye toward David, her son leaned close to her ear and whispered, "He's bad news like Joey."

Chapter Four

"Mitch Blackburn is Joey's brother?" Lisa's gaze fastened onto the teenager under discussion.

"Yes, Joey's always bragging about how Mitch would skip school and cheat on tests when he was in high school and how last year he dropped out." Andy's voice was so low she could hardly hear him. He didn't look at Mitch but at David a few feet away.

"Thanks for telling me, hon. I'll keep an eye on him, but you don't need to worry about anything while you're here." She gave Andy a reassuring smile. "I got the feeling Mitch really needed this job, so I think he'll be all right here."

"Sure, Mom. I'm eating in your office if that's okay. I have homework to do." He shuffled toward the back.

She faced the man, quickly closing the space between them. "I'm due for a break so, yeah, I'll have dinner with you but it's my treat." The least she could do was treat him to dinner for taking care of Andy this evening.

"But I—"

She held up her hand to stop his words. "You helped me tonight. Dinner is my thank you."

"The words are enough."

"What would you like?"

He looked at her for a long moment, then switched his attention to the menu on the wall behind the counter. "I'd like a small pizza with everything on it and coffee."

"Grab a table. I'll put our orders in and be there in a minute." How long could she delay sitting down to eat with him? She saw the questions in his eyes. He was curious about what Andy had told her.

After giving the cook the order, Lisa checked on Andy in her office. "What did you tell Coach Russell about the tae kwon do lessons on Saturday?"

Her son glanced up from his history book. "I haven't made up my mind."

"Do you want to do it?"

"He said it would help my game. I should try it. Gabe is gonna do it. Are you really okay about it?"

"Yeah," she murmured, thinking about the times she wished she could have defended herself. Maybe she could get Andy to show her what he learned because she wouldn't have lost Andy to the state if she had been able to protect him from her boyfriend. Or she could find an adult class to take or David could show her. She gulped at the thought. "If you need me, I'll be out front at a table eating with Coach Russell."

His face blank, Andy buried his head in his book. She stayed by the door for a few extra seconds, trying to gauge his reaction to her eating with David. Andy's narrowed gaze and rigid stance proclaimed he was still leery of the police. Her son's attention remained glued to the page.

Shrugging, Lisa turned away and made her way toward the front, stopping briefly to get a cup of black coffee for David and a glass of ice water for herself. She slipped into the chair across from him and slid the mug toward him. "How did practice go today?"

David cradled the coffee between his large hands and stared at the black liquid. "Okay. There's still tension on the team but nothing overt. The parents I talked to concerning the fight followed up at home with their children. Joey's the only one whose parents I couldn't get in contact with. I've left several messages."

"Joey's father hasn't returned them?"

"No, but Andy said something about Joey's brother being here. I'll say something to him before I leave to have his father call me. It's likely Joey is erasing the messages. Hopefully his brother will deliver it."

"That might work," Lisa said, but doubt laced her words. Remembering what Andy told her about Mitch made her question her newest employee. Had Joey learned everything from his older brother?

David's gaze drifted toward the counter, then back to her. "Andy seemed upset when he was talking about Joey's brother."

"He doesn't think Mitch is the right kind of employee for the restaurant. I told Andy I would keep an eye on Joey's brother."

"Do you think your son is right?"

"Mitch hasn't given me any reason to question him as an employee. He's worked here a week and done a good job."

"I wonder if that's the same guy who's been picking Joey up at practice when he doesn't get a ride with one of his friends."

Lisa scanned the restaurant, leaned across the table and said, "Mitch just walked back behind the counter and is talking to Nathan at the cash register."

"That could be the same guy. It was hard to see him clearly. When I tried to catch him, he would leave in a hurry. The car was full of other teens."

"Mitch's friends, probably."

"Two of the three other teens were young, not much older than Joey. That seems odd to me."

She cocked her head to the side. "Do you question everyone's actions?"

"You've accused me of being too suspicious, and I guess I am. I have a hard time turning off the cop when I clock off the job. Mitch looks to be about eighteen. Most that age don't hang out with thirteen- or fourteen-year-olds."

"Mitch is nineteen. So you think I should fire him because he has younger kids in his car? Maybe they're cousins, neighbors or even a brother of the other older teen in the car."

"I'm not saying that. But your son might be right. At least keep a close eye on Mitch."

"I will, but I can't fire someone for no reason."

"No, but be careful. Joey learned his behavior from someone." David stared at Mitch for a moment, then returned his gaze to Lisa, concern in his eyes. "I didn't say anything to the guys today, but Vic Parson called me earlier to tell me he can't continue coaching for health reasons."

"So you're it."

"Yeah, unless you want to help out."

She laughed. "I can blow a whistle, but that's the extent of my expertise as a basketball coach."

His mouth tilted up in a grin. "I figured that. Any suggestions for someone to help me?"

"I know I've seen Jacob and Roman playing basketball with some of the foster kids on the outside court at the refuge. Maybe one of them would help you."

"When I'm at Stone's Refuge this weekend, I'll check with both of them. With my job, there may be times I won't be able to make practice or for that matter a game, so I'll need at least one assistant."

"Maybe both of them will do it."

"That would be even better." David took a long sip of his drink. "Did Andy tell you if he would be joining the class? After talking with him on the ride, I didn't say anything else to him about it. I don't want him to feel pressured."

"I think he's gonna do it, especially because Gabe is."

"Yeah, I talked with Gabe today, and he was excited about the class. He immediately got Terry signed up and a few others. It should be a nice size class."

"Terry is Andy's other best friend at the refuge. They all stick together."

Nathan approached the table with two pizzas, steam wafting off them. The delicious aroma reminded her how hungry she was. After thanking him, she bowed her head and said a blessing, then scooped up her first slice of black olives, feta cheese, tomatoes, peppers and bacon.

"I didn't realize how hungry I was until now." Lisa washed her bite down with a swallow of water.

"I skipped lunch, so this is welcomed."

"What? Working too hard you can't take some time for something to eat?"

"Actually I've been working on a case involving a new gang that hits an area—homes and businesses—then moves on to another part of town just as we close in on them."

"Where have they robbed?"

"The last area is northeast, not far from the interstate."

"There are some nice homes in that part of town."

"Yeah, and there are some homeowners who are upset, not to mention the owners of a hair salon and coffee shop."

"No leads?"

"A few." David popped the last part of his slice into his mouth.

"Should I be concerned?" Lisa waved her hand to indicate the restaurant.

His gaze swept the dining room. "So far with this gang they've struck only small businesses when things have been slow—few people around, and from what I've heard and seen, this place is busy. I doubt you have much downtime. With the homes, they strike during the day when the people are gone. Thankfully no one has been hurt, but that could always change." He caught her look, a fervor in his eyes. "But you should always be concerned and alert."

"How many?"

"Three. They wear ski masks, so we don't have a description."

She nodded her head toward him. "Consider me warned." Listening to him talk about the robbery gang underlined the type of people he had to deal with day in and day out. Getting him involved in the refuge would be a good thing to give him a balance in what he saw of life. He needed that.

Lisa parked her Chevy in front of the recreational center at Stone's Refuge on Saturday morning. "I'm going to see Hannah, but I'll try to get back here to see the end of your class."

"Ah, Mom, you don't have to. I'm not even sure I'll stay."

"I thought you were going to try it."

Andy thrust his shoulders back. "I'm only doing it because Gabe and Terry are. I don't need it to make my basketball game better." He pushed open his door and hopped from the car.

Lisa watched him hurry into the rec hall. Lately she'd been seeing a lot of his back as he rushed from her. As though he were hiding something from her. That thought brought a frown to her face. She remembered David's words about why would Andy be hiding what was really going on between him and

Joey. Was it more than Joey bullying her son because Andy was doing well in class?

She slipped from her Chevy and headed toward Hannah's house, a crispness still clinging to the early morning air. In the pasture some trees had lost their leaves, but many proclaimed the season with bright orange-red, canary yellow or dark red leaves. The beauty of them lifted her spirits. With the Lord's help she would find a way to reach her son.

Hannah answered her knock almost immediately. Before her friend could greet her, both her adopted sons, Gabe and Terry, shot around her and darted down the steps, then ran toward the recreational center.

"They seem excited about the class," Lisa said as she entered Hannah's house.

"Not only are they excited about learning tae kwon do, but a police officer is teaching them. They think that's a big deal." Hannah shut her front door. "Let's go into the kitchen. I actually have some quiet time because Jacob took the girls to the barn to see the new colt."

"That's all Andy talks about is Tiger."

"Why did they name the colt Tiger?"

"Because Andy is such a huge fan of the University of Cimarron's basketball team, the Tigers. I promised him some time this season I would take him to a game. I was thinking about getting some tickets for a game as a Christmas gift. I still can't believe it's a month away. I'm not ready for the holidays."

"I'm never ready." In the kitchen Hannah filled two cups with coffee and then sat at the table. "Have you seen Whitney and Kelli this morning?"

"If Andy decides to take this class, we're gonna rearrange our Saturday get-together to lunch instead of breakfast."

"You don't have to. Andy can spend the night with us Friday and go over with my sons."

"I'd rather bring him and pick him up."

While Hannah took a sip of her drink, she looked long and hard at Lisa. "Why? Does this have anything to do with the teacher?"

Lisa stared at her milk-flavored coffee, trying to find a way to explain her conflicting emotions concerning David Russell. "Have you ever thought the Lord brought you into someone's life for a purpose, to help them?"

Her friend grinned. "Yes, you. The day I met you I knew in my heart you loved your son very much, and I wanted to help you find a way to be a part of Andy's life."

"I don't know what I would have done without your intervention. And there's something about David that calls to me, and yet Andy doesn't want to have anything to do with him because he's a police officer. Frankly that makes me hesitate, too."

"You're not that person you were four years ago. You've changed so much."

"Yeah, well, David doesn't feel people can change really."

"Have you told him about your past?"

Lisa ran a finger around the rim of her mug, the heat of her drink caressing her palm. "No, and if we continue to get to know each other, I feel I should and that conversation isn't one I want to have with David. I haven't hidden my past, but neither am I proud of what I did."

"Why do you think you have to tell him?"

"Because it isn't a secret, and I don't want him hearing from anyone but me. He doesn't have a lot of faith in the human race. I don't want him to think I purposely set out to hide my past from him."

"Again I'm still not sure why you feel the need to reveal something that has nothing to do with the person you are today.

I don't go around telling people about my past when I meet them. They don't get that privilege until I get to know them well. Do you care for him as more than a casual acquaintance?"

The heat of a blush suffused Lisa's face. "I feel as though the Lord wants me to help David return to Him. I can't shake that feeling. I can't do that with anything between us."

"You haven't really answered my question. How do *you* really feel about him?"

Lisa fluttered her hand in the air. "With my past experience I haven't done well in that department. My son should be my life now. But I like David—probably more than I should."

"Andy is twelve. What are you going to do when he leaves home after high school?"

"I'm enjoying my job, especially with my new responsibilities. The restaurant is doing great. When I took over as manager, it didn't fall apart."

Hannah's eyebrows shot up. "You thought that would happen?"

"Yes."

Her friend leaned forward. "Well, I've got news for you. You worked hard for that promotion. Give yourself the credit that's due."

Lisa chuckled. "Okay. I get your point." Taking a swallow of her now-lukewarm coffee, she checked the wall clock and put her mug on the table. "I'd better head back to the rec hall. I want to catch some of the class."

"Who are you checking up on—Andy or David?"

"Both." Lisa stood and took her half-filled mug to the sink. "For all I know my son is sitting in the car or watching the class waiting for me."

"Or he's enjoying himself and has forgotten about leaving."

"I'm hoping for the latter, but with Andy lately, I don't know what's going on with him."

"That's being a teenager." Hannah walked with her to the door.

"He's not officially a teen for another six months."

On the way back to the recreation hall Lisa thought about what they had discussed. If she stayed away from David, then she wouldn't have to say a word to him about her past. But with all the Lord had done for her, if He wanted her to help David, how could she turn her back on Him or David?

Who are you kidding? You want to help David like he's trying to help you with Andy.

Inside she slipped into a chair, pleased that Andy hadn't been in the car or sitting out watching the others going through the exercises David was having them do. In fact, her son was at the front of the group of boys between Gabe and Terry, following everything that David was showing them.

At the end David had different students come up and demonstrate the moves they learned that day. Andy did a leg kick for the group. When David indicated it was done well, Andy gave him a half grin that quickly vanished when her son caught sight of her.

After the class bowed to David, he dismissed them. Andy ambled toward her. Although he wasn't frowning, he wasn't smiling either. In the past she'd become quite good at telling what her son was thinking almost before he did, but lately he was becoming accomplished at hiding his feelings from her. If she hadn't caught that half smile a few moments ago, she would have thought he didn't really like the class.

"Gabe told me Belle has finally got milk for Tiger. Can I go with Gabe to the barn and see the colt? Roman is over there. I want to make sure they don't need me to feed Tiger anymore."

"Sure." Andy started to turn away and Lisa hurriedly asked, "Are you gonna continue taking this class?"

"Yeah. Gabe is. I might as well." Andy glimpsed his best friend at the door and hurried toward him.

"He seemed to get into it."

David's deep baritone voice took her by surprise. She whirled around and faced him. "I'm glad."

"What did you think?"

"They all were focused on what you were doing. That's a good thing with adolescents."

"I think this is going to be a nice class. Roman's wife stopped by and asked if I could do a class for some of the girls. I'm going to see what I can do, but we'll start having basketball games in two weeks, so my time will be limited for a while."

"Have you asked Roman or Jacob about helping you coach?"

"Not yet, but the boys were talking before class, and I understand both of them are at the barn with Peter. Something about planning a barn raising for next weekend."

In all that had been going on in her life, she'd forgotten about what Peter and Roman wanted to do to expand the facilities for the animals. "After almost five years they need more space. Actually they needed it a year ago, but building the rec hall and fifth cottage were more important for the children in foster care."

"I'm gonna volunteer to help with the barn raising. I'll be here anyway teaching the class next Saturday. How about you?"

"I figure I can use a hammer—maybe. If not, I'll help with the food preparation for the workers. I know that Hannah and Whitney are in charge of that."

David started toward the door, the hall empty of children. "Are you going to the barn now?"

"Yeah. I have to leave soon and I need to take Andy home."

"Are you working?"

"No, meeting Whitney and your sister for lunch."

The sunrays bathed the landscape in warmth as Lisa ducked under the fence into the pasture between the refuge and the barn.

Easily falling into step beside David, she slanted a look toward the man who towered next to her. "Andy said something about you had a chance to play pro ball and didn't take it. He couldn't believe you would turn down the offer. He dreams of two things, being a basketball player and a vet. He intends to do both."

"It didn't fit into my plans. It got me a scholarship to college, but I didn't want to make basketball my life."

"So you became a cop."

Silence hung between them for several yards before David slowed his pace, his gaze on her. "Yeah. That was my dream."

A look in his eyes held a flash of pain until he quickly masked it, but the brief glimpse bothered her. She didn't want to care. "That doesn't sound like your dream now."

"Reality has a way of waking up a person."

"Do you wish now you had taken the offer to be a pro player?"

He shook his head.

She dragged her gaze from his and focused on the barn. "What would you have done if you hadn't been a police officer?"

"A teacher maybe. I enjoyed teaching the boys today."

She came to a halt, swinging around to face him. "Interesting. I didn't expect that."

A grin tugged at one corner of his mouth. "What did you expect?"

"Oh, I don't know. Maybe a lawyer or some kind of businessman."

"Why?"

She shrugged, not sure why. "I guess I could see you as a PE teacher."

"My major was in science."

"You're full of surprises today. I wouldn't have pictured you as a scientist."

He waggled his eyebrows. "Not even a mad scientist?"

She laughed. "Well, maybe at least the mad part."

His chuckle prompted her to resume her trek toward the barn. He quickly caught up her, snagging her hand in his.

Surprised by the action, Lisa blurted out the first thing that came to mind. "You know if you want to quit the police force you could always be a teacher. I've heard Peter complaining about the shortage of teachers, especially in math and science."

"I'll keep that in mind if I decide to change professions."

"Or you could teach tae kwon do." Walking across a field with a guy holding her hand wasn't something she'd ever done. The gesture heightened her awareness of not only him but everything around her—the scent of the cool air with a hint of burning wood as if someone was using their fireplace, the sound of the birds chirping and a flock of geese flying overhead south, the feel of moisture beading on her upper lip because she was nervous.

"Unless I open a gym I doubt I can make much doing that."

"Yeah, true. I could use a gym. I need to get in better shape. My walking/jogging isn't working so good."

He paused at the edge of the yard in front of the barn, releasing her hand and facing her. "Maybe you need inspiration."

She shielded her eyes from the bright sunlight with her hand and looked up at him. "Like what? A scale posted on my fridge?"

He chuckled. "I was thinking more along the line of someone to jog with."

"I suppose I could ask Whitney or Hannah again. Or maybe your sister."

His chuckle evolved into a full belly laugh. "Kelli? She hates to exercise. How about me?"

"You!" Her voice squeaked, announcing to the whole world—okay, only David—just how nervous she was. She didn't date much—correction, hadn't in years—not that jogging together was considered a date. "You would leave me in your dust."

"I promise I won't. I'll inspire you to pick up the speed." He waggled his eyebrows.

She burst out laughing. "I'm gonna accept just to see how you're gonna do that."

He resumed his walk toward the barn. "Diplomatically, of course. We can do it a couple of times a week first thing in the morning before either one of us has to go to work. Give it a try this Monday, and if you don't like it, then we don't have to continue."

"Okay."

Hannah's daughter, Emily, emerged from the barn and raced toward her clutching a pair of sunglasses. Jacob quickly came out, slowing his pace when he saw Lisa not far away. Giggling, the toddler kept going and threw herself into her arms.

"Are you running away?" Lisa asked, twirling the child around, the sound of her laughter sprinkling the air. If she had her life to do over, she'd have a ton of kids.

Emily pointed toward Jacob. "Dad-dee after me."

Jacob stopped in front of Lisa, fixing a stern expression on his face although his eyes twinkled. "Miss Emily, do you have my glasses?"

The toddler nodded and thrust it into her father's hands as he reached toward her.

"I'd better go get Andy." Lisa used Jacob's appearance to put some distance between her and David.

As she entered the barn, she peered back at the two men still talking in the middle of the pasture, Jacob holding a wiggling child. Jacob nodded then started across the field to his house. She and David were going to jog together on Monday. When she had begun walking/jogging, she had wanted a partner to keep her motivated to go when she didn't want to, which was most mornings. When Hannah and Whitney had declined because their schedules didn't jell with hers, it had been easier just to let go the idea of a partner. Now she had one and the fact made her smile.

She saw Roman and made her way toward the vet, standing near the pen of puppies. "Have you seen Andy?"

"Up until five minutes ago he was right here playing with the puppies."

"Which way did he go?"

Roman pointed toward the back entrance. "He's with Gabe. They both wanted to check on Tiger in the paddock behind the barn."

"Thanks."

Outside she scanned the area and found Tiger near Belle but no Andy and Gabe. She started to shout her son's name when she heard raised voices—one being Andy's. She headed toward the sound at the side of the barn.

A few steps away from the corner, Andy still not visible, she heard Gabe say, "If you think he's doing that, you need to tell your mom. Joey's bad news."

Joey? Alert, she came to a stop, just short of rounding the corner.

"I can't. I don't have any proof."

Proof? Of what? As Lisa flattened herself against the barn, she discovered David not two feet behind her. From the grim expression on his face, he'd obviously overheard what her son had said, too. Oh, great!

"You know what happens to snitches," Andy said, fear in his voice.

Snitches? Alarmed, Lisa stepped in view of the two boys. "Andy, Gabe, what are you talking about?"

Andy opened his mouth to say something, but his gaze flew to a spot behind her. He clamped his lips together and lowered his head. She didn't have to glance behind her to know that David had appeared. Her body tingled with awareness of the man standing a few feet away from her.

"I want an answer. What kind of proof? Why would you be a snitch?" The only thing that came to her mind involved drugs, which sent her heartbeat galloping.

Andy lifted his head and stabbed her with a mutinous glare. "Mom, I told you I'm gonna take care of it. Joey's cheating."

The few times Andy lied to her she could tell because he blinked more than usual. This time he didn't. Was that what was bothering him or was it something more? "Why should Joey's cheating concern you?"

Andy shrugged. "It just does. It's not right. Besides, it throws off the class curve."

"I need to go. I promised Dad I would help him rake leaves this afternoon." Gabe spun on his heel and hurried away.

"If something happens that's wrong, you need to speak up, Andy."

His eyes narrowed. "I can't accuse someone if I don't have proof." He stormed past Lisa and went in the opposite direction from his friend.

Lisa started to follow.

"Cheating isn't the problem. You do know that, don't you?" David's question halted her steps. She rounded on him. "Stay out of my business."

"This may be my business."

She put her hand on her waist. "My son has done nothing wrong to warrant the police."

Surprise flickered into David's eyes. "I was talking as a friend and Andy's coach, not a cop." He rubbed his hand along his jawline. "What's going on with Joey may be police business. I've been checking up on Joey and Mitch. Joey lives with his older brother and father. The dad is rarely around, so it's mostly Mitch raising Joey. According to the neighbors, people have been seen coming and going from the house at all hours."

She was almost afraid to ask, but she couldn't ignore it. "So what do you think is going on?"

"Possibly drugs."

He said aloud what she'd been thinking and the very word caused terror to grip her. "Drugs? Andy wouldn't take drugs." Not after what she'd gone through; at least that was what she hoped and prayed. No, she knew her son and she wasn't going to start doubting him because of David Russell.

"How do you know that? Sadly, it's part of our culture, and young people are faced with it all the time." His hand moved to massage his nape. "Maybe it's something else besides drugs. I don't have anything concrete."

"And neither does Andy." Although she was defending her son, she would be talking to him again at home. She had to assure herself drugs weren't involved.

"But he has good instincts. I see it on the court when he's playing ball. He's aware of everyone around him, knows just the right person to throw to. He knows more than he's saying, possibly more than he realizes."

If it was drugs, her worst nightmare had come back to haunt her. *Lord, please don't let it be drugs. I want nothing to do with my old life.*

"What am I supposed to do?" she muttered out loud, then wanted to immediately snatch the question back, but it was there between her and David.

David moved closer, clasping her upper arms. "Let me help you. If Joey is dealing or doing something else illegal, I want to get to the bottom of it. Andy shouldn't have to handle it by himself."

"But what if it's just cheating?"

David's intense blue gaze captured hers. "Do you really believe that?"

She shook her head. The son she knew wouldn't be afraid to confide in her concerning a classmate cheating on tests. She had to acknowledge what she feared since the fight. It might be more than bullying. "If you start interrogating Andy, he'll clam up."

"I know." He drew her into his embrace. The feel of his arms around her gave her assurance she wasn't alone in this. In that moment her feelings toward David shifted into emotionally dangerous territory.

"You said something about a lunch date. I thought I would stay and help Roman and Peter stake out the new barn location because Jacob got called away. I can bring Andy home later."

"What's your plan?"

"I'm going to win his trust. Be someone he'll feel safe with."

"That might not be possible."

"Why?"

"Because you're a cop."

His brow wrinkled, doubt entering in his eyes. "Has he had a run-in with the police before?"

This wasn't the time or the place to tell him about her past, but she would have to soon if she continued to see him. "No, he's never been in trouble with the law." She cocked her head to the side. "Why do you want to do this?"

Chapter Five

To atone for another child's death. For a brief moment David had wanted to say that to Lisa, but that was a secret he would keep buried and deal with privately. "I went into law enforcement to help," he said, his standard response, but he stuffed his hands into his pockets to keep their trembling hidden. The thought of the child he killed shook his core and threatened him anew.

Lisa checked her watch. "I need to get going. Let me find Andy and tell him."

"Do me a favor. Tell Roman Andy is gonna get a ride to his house with me." He forced nonchalance into his stance and voice that he didn't feel.

She chuckled. "You're devious."

"I promise I won't say anything about drugs or Joey. I want to get to know him and let Andy get to know me. That's all."

"Okay. I trust you."

The words "I trust you" lifted David's spirits. Actually Lisa's presence did. At times, especially when Andy was involved, he'd glimpsed a vulnerability in her that told him she would understand the anguish he'd experienced. And yet, he couldn't bring himself to speak of it out loud.

"Let me find Roman." Lisa rounded the corner of the barn and caught a glimpse of Andy in the far pasture with Tiger and Belle.

In the barn she found Roman in the tack room. "I need to leave. Please let Andy know he's gonna catch a ride home with David."

Roman looked from David to Lisa. "Fine. Andy's out in the south pasture. I had him move Belle and Tiger there."

"I saw him, but I'm running late. See you all later."

As she strode toward the front entrance, she glanced back at David, worry etched into her features. She was concerned about Andy and rightly so. He had a gut feeling it was a lot worse than cheating. He would be there for her, if she would allow it.

When she disappeared from view, David decided to fill Roman in. Not the reason behind wanting to get to know Andy, but that he wanted to spend some time with the twelve-year-old.

"I understand. Lisa is a special lady," Roman said after David's explanation.

"Yeah." The twinkle in the vet's gaze made David quickly say, "but we're just friends. Nothing else." He was damaged goods with a life barely held together. He wasn't even sure if he should remain a police officer.

"Sure. That's what I said when I was dating Cathy."

"But that's the truth."

"That's what I thought, too, and I suppose we were friends first. But somewhere along the line, I realized my buddies were right. There was much more between us." A shadow drove the twinkle from Roman's eyes.

"Is something wrong?"

"The doctor can't seem to find what's ailing my wife. She's going back to him, and I'm sure he'll run more tests."

"I'm sorry to hear that. I saw her this morning right before class. She wanted me to form one for the girls."

"That sounds like Cathy." Roman hefted the toolbox. "Are you ready to stake where the new barn is going?"

"Yep. Let me get Andy. He can help us."

"Good because everyone is deserting me. Peter had to go back to the house, too. Something about the washer overflowing."

David loped out to the south pasture. Andy watched him approach, a wariness taking over his expression and stance. All casualness was gone. By the time David arrived in front of him, the child stood stiffly, his mouth firmed in a fierce line as though he were preparing to do battle.

"Roman was hoping you would help us with staking out the new barn location. Something came up with Peter and Jacob."

"Where's Mom?"

David hadn't wanted a confrontation about him taking Andy home, but suspicion leaked into the child's voice, and he knew Andy would force the issue of how he was getting home. "She had to meet some friends. She mentioned a Saturday get-together."

"When is she coming back?"

"She's not." David hadn't thought it possible that the kid could get any more rigid but he did.

Andy fisted his hands at his sides and straightened his shoulders. "How am I getting home?" he asked in a tone honed razor sharp.

"Me. C'mon. Let's go help Roman." David turned to leave. When Andy didn't move, David glanced back. "Coming?"

Confusion greeted his question. Andy's brows furrowed, but his mouth eased its hard line. "I'll be there."

David jogged back toward the barn, glimpsing the boy throwing his arms around the colt's neck and whispering something to him. As David went into the cavernous structure, Andy trudged across the pasture. It was going to be a long day. What had caused such wariness in the child? How was he going to reach Andy and get to the bottom of what was going on if the boy was always defensive and leery of everything he said? He wished he had answers to those questions, but he was lost. No wonder he wasn't a parent.

"What did you think of the class today?" David made another attempt at conversation with Andy on the drive back into town from the ranch. Most of the afternoon the boy had been sulking or talking with Roman and ignoring most of what he said.

And for a long moment David thought Andy was going to continue to ignore him, but suddenly in the quiet the child answered, "That's all Gabe talked about on the way to the barn afterward. He's looking forward to next Saturday." He shifted in his seat, facing David. "We are gonna have class before the barn raising, aren't we?"

"Yeah. I thought I would call Hannah and let her know we'll start an hour earlier, though. So you're coming next week, then?" He glanced toward Andy.

The boy sat forward, staring out the windshield. "Sure, why not. All my friends are in it."

"I could use your help."

Silence.

Again David threw a look toward Andy as he entered the outskirts of Cimarron City. The child's mouth pinched into a frown. "If you think I need to explain a move better, I'd like you to tell me. Sometimes I tend to hurry, assume everyone understands what I'm saying." He grinned. "That may not always be the case. So will you?"

The child's frown relaxed into a neutral expression. "Yeah."

For a few seconds David held his gaze until Andy averted his head. "Thanks. I want this to work out."

In more ways than one. He needed to get closer to Andy. If

he couldn't break through the barrier Andy had around himself, he might never discover what was going on with him and Joey. The thought of the conversation between Gabe and Andy earlier constricted his stomach. He was ninety percent sure it centered around drugs. He'd talk with a few guys in narcotics and see what they thought, especially concerning a Mitch Blackburn. Was he a player? Was Joey involved?

"What did Roman mean at the end about seeing you on Monday afternoon at the gym? Is he coming to our practice?"

"He's the new assistant coach. I needed someone to help me out. And Jacob will fill in when one of us has to be gone."

"Oh, that's good. The guys will like them."

He wanted so badly to ask Andy about Joey and what he and Gabe had been arguing about earlier, but David bit the inside of his mouth to keep the question to himself. Andy was talking to him, which was a step forward from earlier at the ranch.

Silence fell between them. David searched for a topic that Andy would discuss.

"Our first game is in two weeks. The Spartans are a tough team to beat. I understand they won the league championship last year," David finally said, only a few blocks away from the apartment complex where Lisa lived.

"Do you think we'll be ready by then?"

"It depends. We aren't really playing as a team yet. I thought I would ask the guys to help out at the barn raising next weekend as a team-building activity. What do you think?"

Andy shrugged. "Some might, but I doubt Joey and his friends would."

"Good point. I'll have to think about it." Maybe he could present it as something that was required. "Jacob mentioned a lot of the kids at the refuge play. Maybe we could get a game going afterward. See how we play with a little competition."

David pulled into a parking space in front of the apartment building where Andy lived.

"Might work." The boy gripped the handle, and as soon as David turned off the engine, Andy jumped out of the Jeep and hurried up the stairs to his apartment.

David exited his car and pocketed his keys. The twelve-year-old disappeared inside his place. At a slower pace David climbed the stairs and started to ring the bell when Lisa flung the front door open.

"How did it go? Andy made a beeline for his bedroom. He didn't have much to say." She stepped out onto the landing, shared by another apartment unit.

"Fine, after he got into the swing of things."

She smiled, her blue eyes lighting up as though the sun shone on water. "How long did that take?"

"Actually not too long. We even talked on the ride home."

"About Joey?" The grin vanished.

"No, about basketball."

Lisa ran her hand back and forth along the metal railing. "Oh, good. Do you want to come in for some coffee?"

He shrank the space between them on the landing and took her hands. "We'll figure out what's going on with Andy and Joey." He cocked a grin. "After all, I'm a top-notch detective. Surely I can gather the clues and put it all together."

"Andy is a good kid." Tears blurred her eyes and she dropped her head so she wasn't looking at him.

He lifted her chin with his finger, said, "I know," then kissed her forehead before moving toward the stairs. "See you Monday morning. Let's meet at Johnson Park at seven."

Weak-kneed, Lisa watched David descend the stairs and start for his Jeep sitting in the parking lot. She clutched the railing while the sound of his car's engine roared to life. His lips left a burning brand on her brow. His declaration she wasn't alone in this situation with Andy still rang in her ears.

If Joey was somehow involved in drugs, she didn't want Andy mixed up in a situation that had to do with drugs. She knew the dangers and lure for some and what those people would do to protect themselves. Was that why Andy wasn't talking to her about his problems with Joey? Because of her drug history? He would want to shield her from anything having to do with her old habit. That made sense to her and also reinforced the need to get to the bottom of what was going on. But she wasn't alone. David would help her.

Please, Lord, watch over my son and help me to find out what's really happening between Andy and Joey.

Sucking in gasping breaths, Lisa plopped onto the bench in Johnson Park Monday morning, crunching up her mouth in a frown. "I see your game, David Russell." She drew in more deep gulps of air until her lungs stopped burning. "You push me to jog more than walk, then at the end challenge me to a race. I got news for you. I ain't going any farther than this seat for at least the next fifteen minutes."

David ran in place the whole time she made her announcement, a huge grin on his face. "I'm proud of you."

She shielded her eyes from the glare of the sun over his left shoulder and looked up at him. "Are you daft? I'm not moving. What's there to be proud of?"

He slowed, going through some stretches while checking his watch. "Because you jogged for twenty minutes straight. That's great for someone who professes to do more walking than jogging."

"I did?" She glanced at her own watch. "I did! I guess time does fly by when you're miserable."

Stopping, he laughed. "I think I was insulted."

"Just think? That was for challenging me to a race."

He folded his long length beside her on the suddenly very small bench in front of the pond at the park. "I was teasing you."

"You have a weird sense of humor. I didn't find anything funny about it."

"You followed everything I said. I was wondering when you'd have enough of that."

"Guess you found out."

"Now we have something to build on. If you can do twenty minutes today. You can do twenty-one tomorrow."

"Tomorrow! No way. I'm taking a day of rest. All the articles I've read about exercising say three times a week. That's my limit."

"That's a minimum, not a maximum."

"Maybe for you. Not me." Lisa pointed across the street. "Hey, I see a doughnut shop. I'm hungry and thirsty."

"There's got to be a better place than a doughnut shop around here." David scanned the strip mall. "Okay, maybe not."

"I thought cops loved dough—"

"Don't say it, Lisa Morgan." His mockingly stern look blasted her, but beneath the expression amusement seeped through.

"Can we go over there and get something to drink at least?"

"Okay. Maybe they have some juice." He rose and held his hand out to her.

She slipped her within his, and he tugged her up with more strength then needed. She crashed into him and sent him flying back with her following. She ended up on top of him as he lay sprawled in the brown grass.

Laughter crinkled the corners of his eyes. "Sorry. I forgot how small you were."

"Small. I could kiss you for that." The second she said it

she bit her bottom lip to keep her mouth shut. Heat flooded her face that had nothing to do with exercising. "I mean, you think I'm small."

"Yeah, you're a foot shorter than me," he said with a straight face.

"Oh, you mean height-wise."

He rolled her to the side, and leaped to his feet in one motion and scooped her up. "You weigh practically nothing." He set her in front of him.

On impulse she rose on tiptoes and planted a kiss on his cheek, then quickly scooted back. "I may have you repeat that a couple of times a day."

His chuckles vied with the sound of cars on the street nearby. "Let's go get you some sustenance." He took her hand and started toward the doughnut shop. "If you want to do it only three times a week, then let's meet on Monday, Wednesday and Friday. Okay?"

"A regular routine?"

"That's the best way to get into the rhythm of exercising. Of course with winter approaching weather may interfere some days."

Lisa managed to jog across the street and entered the parking lot of the strip mall. David talked as though this was a long-term partnership. Maybe it was safer to say gig as jogging buddies. Yeah, that was probably much safer. And yet, in spite of not caring much for exercising, she found herself looking forward to Wednesday.

The sounds of hammers striking wood and saws buzzing finally stopped. Lisa positioned herself behind a long table laden with sandwiches, chips, pieces of fruit and various desserts—cookies, bars and a sheet cake. Thirty yards away the second barn stood, its frame up and one side completely done.

"Here comes the onslaught," Whitney said, putting out the paper napkins for the crew erecting the barn.

At the opposite end of the table, Lisa finished cutting slices of the pumpkin spice cake. "I figured Andy would be at the front of the line for food. He's gotta be going through a growth spurt."

"I think Gabe is, too," Hannah said next to Lisa. "I'm glad David has his team here. The kids have been wonderful about cleaning up, fetching supplies for the men, hammering boards." She leaned close to Lisa. "And my sons are looking forward to beating them at basketball later. That's all they've been talking about at the refuge, the big game later."

"I was surprised he announced at the end of the practice Monday that the boys had to be here today. There were a few who grumbled they had plans, but most were eager to prove themselves on the court and to help out. I've seen a few sneak away to pet the animals."

Lisa searched the crowd flocking to the food tables and found Joey hanging back with two of his friends. She'd been keeping an eye on him because David was busy scaling the rafters in the new barn and working on putting the roof on the structure. Once Joey had seen her watching him and gave her a cocky grin, then tipped an imagery hat.

As the child in question came down the food line, he paused in front of her. "I'm sorry about that night after practice a few weeks ago. Andy and me just had a misunderstanding. It won't happen again."

His innocent expression didn't fool Lisa. He was up to something. "What did you two fight about?" She was curious to see if the boy would say the same thing Andy had.

"No big deal." Joey moved toward the end of the line, his friend behind him whispering something in his ear. Joey laughed, sliding his glance toward her.

Chilled, she turned to serve a piece of cake to the person who had paused in front of her. Another cocky grin flashed in front of her.

David leaned across the table. "Keeping an eye on a certain young man?"

"Yes."

He straightened. "I have been, too. I've got a great view up there." He pointed toward the top of the barn. "I won't let anything happen to Andy if I can help it."

"I know." His musky scent enveloped her, shrinking the space between them. The temperature seemed to soar. "Do you want some pumpkin spice cake?"

"Did you make it?"

"Yes."

"I'll take a huge piece. I love pumpkin cake, cheesecake, pie. You name it. If it has pumpkin in it, I love it. That's probably why I love Thanksgiving. How about you?"

"I wouldn't have made the cake if I didn't like pumpkin."

"No, I meant do you like Thanksgiving."

"It's okay." With only her and Andy, the holidays could be lonely. She did her best to make it a family affair.

"Turkey and dressing are right up there with pumpkin."

"I usually get only a roasting hen for Andy and me."

"You and Andy should come to Kelli's to have Thanksgiving dinner. She goes all out. I came last year and really look forward to this one."

She noticed several people skirting David and continuing to move down the table. "I don't think—"

"I know Kelli wouldn't mind. She usually has a few people connected with the shelter at her house for Thanksgiving. Besides, you two are friends. She would insist." He gave her a heart-melting smile. "I'd love for you to say yes."

When he was grinning like that, he was impossible to resist. She scooped up a piece of cake and plopped it on his paper plate. "Fine, we'll be there if it's okay with Kelli and Andy is all right with it."

He winked. "I'll charm him into agreeing."

"That I've got to see." Especially knowing her son's feelings toward the police, although they had warmed lately.

"You'll see this will be a great Thanksgiving."

"I'm more into Christmas. Thanksgiving means it's only a month away. Which means right now it's only six weeks away. Eek! I still have so much to do."

"I can do without Christmas."

"You two chitchat some other time. Some of us would like to have the pumpkin cake, too," Roman said with a grin next to David.

David sidled down the line, also snatching up several cookies and an apple to go with his turkey and Swiss sandwich and potato chips.

When everyone was finally settled with their food, Lisa grabbed a plate and filled it. When she scoured the area for a place to eat, David waved at her to join him at a card table. She seriously thought about eating with Andy and his friends under an oak tree to see if she could find out anything, but that probably wouldn't go over too well. Taking the only available chair, she sat with David to eat her lunch. Thankfully Hannah and her husband, Jacob, were at the table, too.

"Just so you know, I'm coaching the refuge team later this afternoon, and yours is going to lose—big time," Jacob said to David.

"Traitor. You're one of our assistant coaches."

Jacob's chuckles set the mood at the table. "Yeah, that's why I'm coaching the other team."

"To throw the game. We need a challenge."

Jacob shook his head. "No way would I ever throw a game, but I'm going to make sure you have that challenge your team needs in order to win against the Spartans next weekend. We're going to beat you all."

"Yeah, we'll just see about that." David popped a chip into his mouth. "When my star player is hot, he is hot."

"Who? Andy? We'll take care of him. I know him well. I taught him everything he knows." Jacob picked up his ham and cheese sandwich.

"I haven't seen too many his age make the three-point shot consistently. You are going down—big time." David punched the air with his forefinger to emphasize the last two words.

Hannah made a *T* with her hands. "Time out. The competition hasn't started. Wait until later."

Jacob bent forward. "Okay, I have to admit Andy is good, but I'll deny it if you tell the kids I said so before the game."

The compliments flying across the small table concerning her son pleased Lisa. Andy loved the game, and if it gave him some success, she hoped that would help him have a better school experience than she had. She could still remember hating school so much because of those girls bullying her that she looked for ways to stay away. She didn't want that for Andy. His academics were his ticket to a better life—if kids like Joey didn't ruin it for him.

Nancy, Hannah's adopted older daughter, approached, holding Emily in her arms. A frown made Nancy appear several years older than her age of ten. "Mom, look what Emily found on the ground. She thought it was candy and was about to eat it." The child presented Hannah with a small pink oblong pill.

Hannah took it and examined it, then passed it to her husband. "Are you familiar with anything that looks like this?"

Jacob paled. "I think it's an antidepressant. Where did she find it?"

Lisa stiffened. What was a prescription antidepressant doing lying around on the ground?

Nancy handed Emily to her mother. "I followed her into the old barn as some boys were leaving. I spoke to them and then caught up with Emily who had picked the pill up off the ground where the boys had been talking."

"Who were the boys in the barn?" David asked, an intensity pouring off him.

"The only one I know the name of is Ryan in cottage three and Andy." Nancy tapped her finger against her chin. "I think the others are on your basketball team."

"How many others?" David gripped his bottle of water so tightly his knuckles whitened.

"Three." The girl snapped her fingers. "Hey, I remember one boy calling one of them Joey. Does that help?"

"Yes, thanks. Please don't say anything to anyone about what your sister found." After taking a gulp of water, David recapped the bottle.

Joey. The name set off alarm bells in Lisa's brain. Joey and his friends might be involved with drugs? Did Andy know something about this? What was her son hiding? A drug problem? She didn't think that was possible. All his life he'd been so against drugs because of what she'd gone through. She'd had to fight him in the past even to take medicine prescribed by Jacob for strep throat. That had been only six months before.

So why was Andy with Joey near where the pill was found by Emily?

"Hon, please watch Emily for a while. I need to talk to your dad." Hannah kissed her toddler, then gave her back to Nancy.

"Emily, don't pick anything up off the ground and eat it. Your sister will get a cookie for you instead."

"Mmm, cook-eee." Emily flung her arms around Nancy's neck as they walked toward the serving tables.

Hannah shifted toward David. "Do you think one of the boys had the pill?"

"Maybe. Selling and taking prescription drugs is growing among teens. That one is one of the drugs of choice. Would Ryan be involved in anything like that?"

Hannah shook her head. "He's eleven. I hope not. I'll have a word with the adults who work in his cottage. Ryan's only been here a few months."

Rising, David gathered his trash, looking straight at Lisa. "It's possible someone with a prescription just accidentally dropped it, but I'm checking the barn out. Make sure there isn't anything else on the ground in there."

After David strode off, Lisa sighed, then drew in a deep, calming breath that did nothing to soothe her. The past conversation left her numb and scared. The questions in David's gaze, directed at her although he hadn't said anything out loud to the others, mirrored the ones she had for her son. What was Andy doing with Joey? Did he know about the antidepressant? Was he taking the drug? How had the pill ended up on the ground in the barn?

"Lisa, are you all right?" Jacob asked, worry in his gaze.

"No. I never wanted to have anything to do with drugs again, especially concerning my son. I don't see Andy doing drugs, but what was he doing in the barn?" Gathering the paper plates and discarded napkins, Lisa stacked them on top of hers.

"Quite the opposite. But you need to find out. I could be wrong." Jacob scrubbed his hand along his jaw. "If you haven't said anything to David about your past, then you need to do it soon. If you're thinking Andy is somehow involved in what's going on, then he does, too. You need to tell him why your son probably would never take any—even prescription ones."

"I haven't yet. But I'm certainly not going to start the conversation unless we're alone and have time to discuss it." Lisa stood, grasping onto the fact none of them believed her son had changed that much to get involved in drugs. She just prayed they were right. "I will but first I'm gonna have a word with Andy. I want to know what's going on between him and Joey once and for all. And I'm not going to accept his explanation it's about grades anymore."

Lisa marched away from the table, searching the crowd for her son. He still sat under the oak tree with Gabe, Terry and a few other boys from his basketball team, finishing his lunch. Trying to school her features into a neutral expression, she covered the short distance between them quickly.

"Andy, I need to talk to you for a moment."

The boys teased Andy about being in trouble and made noises, drawing the attention of others around them. Andy slunk away from the group, his mouth screwed into a frown, his eyes narrowed.

"Emily found an antidepressant pill in the barn on the ground. Right before that Joey was in there with a few boys from the team, you and Ryan."

His expression evolved from a defiant look to one of concern. "Emily. She didn't take it, did she?" Panic edged his voice.

"No, thankfully Nancy saw her pick it up and stopped her."

His tension siphoned from his rigid body, and he sighed heavily. He dropped his gaze to a point between them on the ground.

"What's going on, Andy? Is Joey selling prescription drugs?

Did he try to sell to you? Is that what you've been hiding? Are you involved?"

He jerked his head up, anger hardening his features. "I can't believe you asked me that," he yelled.

Before she could respond, he hurried away. She whirled around to stop him. He was halfway across the yard, heading toward the new, unfinished structure. When she opened her mouth to shout at Andy to come back was the moment she realized that a lot of the people were following their interaction—including David who stood at the entrance into the old barn. His gaze trapped hers for a few seconds before she wrenched it away. It lit upon Gabe whose look was wide-eyed. She hadn't handled the situation well.

She was scared. Scared she was losing her son. Scared Andy was taking drugs. Scared he was mixed up with Joey somehow. *Lord, help me. What do I do?*

She looked toward David, still standing in the entrance. Fury, as though a storm brewed in his blue eyes, carved a hard expression on his face. She was afraid he believed the worse concerning Andy after all that had happened in the past hour. It wasn't true—was it?

She couldn't do this anymore by herself. She needed help. *Lord, help me.*

Chapter Six

What had Andy and Lisa talked about? In the barn entrance, David rolled his shoulders to ease the strain, going through some mental exercises to relax himself. They didn't work. He was wound tight as though he were entering a building where someone was waiting to ambush him. Had Lisa discovered that Andy was somehow involved with drugs to kids? Had there been a falling-out between the two boys over drugs? Or was there something else entirely different going on?

Lisa made her way toward him. The closer she came, the easier it was to see her haunted look. She appeared to be hurting inside and not sure how to fix it. Her expression tugged at him. He didn't want to care about anyone. His own life was barely held together with fragile threads that at any moment would break. But he did care. He ached to hold her to wipe that pain-filled look from her eyes.

Her troubled gaze alerted him to the fact that Lisa must think Andy was somehow connected to the antidepressant dropped in the barn. He didn't want to believe that of Andy, but what else could the kid be hiding?

Trembling with anger at the thought of what could have happened if Emily had chewed the pill, he splayed his fingers wide until they ached. He didn't want to be thrust into a drug situation, especially with kids. That was why he'd become a detective and worked Robbery/Homicide. What if one of the children ended up hurt? How could he deal with that?

The thirteen-year-old he'd killed in the drug deal in Dallas intruded into his thoughts, prodding his guilt to the foreground. Why couldn't he rid himself of that child's image? How long would he pay? But he always came back to wondering what he could have done to prevent killing the adolescent.

He had to remain calm, think like a cop.

He had no evidence that Joey was dealing, and that was what he needed if he was going to protect the kids in his care. He had to break through the barriers Andy had erected between them. Could he trust Lisa to help him?

A few feet from him, Lisa scanned the area before coming to a halt in front of him. "Were there any more pills on the ground?"

He took a step toward her, wanting to wrap her in his embrace and make everything go away. Was Andy involved in something illegal? Tamping down the strong urge, he held his arms taut at his sides. He had a job to do. "Not that I could find." He nodded his head toward the area where she and her son had stood. "Why did Andy stomp off?" He watched first fear, then worry and finally caution flittered into her expression.

"I asked him what was going on with Joey. I wanted to know if he knew Joey was selling drugs."

"I'm gathering he didn't know anything."

"No, but he was really upset about Emily finding the pill."

She wasn't telling him everything. She was leaving something out. What? Was she protecting Andy? She wouldn't be the first parent he'd encountered who had lied to protect her child. He unclenched then clenched his hands over and over, hoping that wasn't the case. He'd begun to trust Lisa these past few weeks—at least trust her as much as he was capable.

"I need to have a word with Roman about Ryan, then get back to work." Maybe he could get something out of the other boy.

"David," Lisa said softly as he started to turn away. "Have you thought that the pill might belong to one of the adults who has a prescription for the drug? Maybe someone accidentally dropped it when getting their medicine out."

"Yup, that crossed my mind for about a second. See you later." He strode toward the unfinished barn in search of Roman and possibly some answers.

He felt the stab of Lisa's look as he crossed the yard. His neck tingled with the anger reaching across the space between them. He didn't have time for niceties, not with the children's safety in question, and if he had stayed a second longer, he would have demanded answers she wasn't willing to give.

The cheering crowd surrounded the outdoor basketball court between cottage one and two at the refuge. Lisa chewed on a fingernail, her nerves taut. The score was close, but Andy's team was winning by four points although he hadn't played well. He'd missed baskets he usually made in the past. Was their conversation earlier affecting his play? Was he feeling guilty about something and that was throwing off his game?

Lisa followed Andy's progress as he broke away from the pack and dribbled toward the hoop at the other end, zigzagging all over the court unnecessarily. Halfway to the basket Andy mishandled the ball, losing control yet again. He stumbled but caught himself before going down. One of the players from the refuge captured the ball and ran with it. Andy started forward, but suddenly halted, swaying.

Lisa straightened. Was he hurt? Her son shook his head, as though clearing it, then began meandering toward his teammates. His erratic movements alerted her.

Something was terribly wrong. If she didn't know better, she would think her child had been drinking or—

She rushed toward him at the same time David did. Five feet away Andy stopped, looked at her with a dazed expression, then collapsed. David managed to get to him to break his fall. Gently he lowered Andy the rest of the way to the concrete and checked his pulse and breathing.

Heart pounding, Lisa hovered over her son. Fear held her motionless. Andy's eyes fluttered close. Her fear quickly evolved into panic. She skirted her son lying still and knelt on the other side of him. "Is he having a seizure?" She frantically searched the crowd about them for Jacob, not sure what to do if that were the case.

"I don't know." David glanced at her with worry in his gaze.

Jacob plowed through the group of boys around them. "Get off the court," he shouted at the kids as he squatted next to her son.

Andy blinked. "Wh-at's wr-wrong?" His words slurred together.

Jacob checked Andy's eyes and vital signs. "Let's take him to the hospital." He looked toward David. "Can you drive? I'll sit in the back with him."

"Yes." David scooped Andy up into his arms and stood. "My car's by the rec hall."

"I'm coming with you," Lisa said, her heart slamming against her chest.

"Of course." David headed toward his vehicle across the compound.

"I'm getting my medical bag. I'll be right there," Jacob called out.

"M-om?"

Lisa matched David's long-legged pace, keeping up with him. "Andy, I'm right here."

"Don't—feel—well." Her son struggled to release each word.

She hurried ahead to open the back door of David's Jeep, then slipped inside. When David reached the vehicle, he leaned in and settled Andy across the seat with his head resting in Lisa's lap. Her son's eyelids flickered, then closed. Her black jeans heightened the pallor of Andy's face.

While David slipped into the front and started the engine, Lisa smoothed Andy's hair from his forehead, her hand quavering so badly even the simplest task seemed difficult.

Lord, please protect Andy.

Jacob squeezed in next to her. "Let's get going," he said to David, then to Lisa Jacob asked, "Is he on any medication?"

"No. He doesn't even like to take anything for his allergies."

"Yeah, I know. I had to check, though." While Jacob was listening to his heartbeat and breathing, Andy opened his eyes again. Jacob paused. "Andy, have you taken anything in the past few hours?"

Her son's forehead furrowed, confusion clouding his eyes. His pupils were large. "On-ly my—" again he blinked slowly as though he were trying to focus on Jacob "—sports dr-ink."

Jacob, and probably David, think Andy's on something. The thought frightened her worse than seeing her son getting attacked by those boys a few weeks ago. *No, it can't be. Not my son. It has to be something else. Please, Lord, not that.*

"What do you think is wrong?" Lisa cradled Andy's head, continuing to stroke his hair back from his forehead.

"Maybe some kind of allergic reaction to something. I'll know more when we get to the hospital and I can run some tests."

Although Jacob appeared calm, his tone professional, it didn't stop her fear from mushrooming. She struggled to take a breath and forced air into her lungs. She had to be strong for Andy.

The Lord is with Andy. The Lord is with me. She kept repeating the words as the distance between the ranch and the hospital shrank.

Wanting to deny the word Jacob was saying, Lisa staggered back a few steps until she encountered the wall of the emergency room. "Andy didn't take antidepressants! He wouldn't!" *Lord, not Andy on drugs. Not my baby.*

"That's what the test results reveal, Lisa. I'm monitoring his blood pressure, breathing and pulse rate. I'm giving him fluids intravenously, and now I'll give him an antidote to counter the benzodiazepine overdose."

Overdose! The word chilled Lisa. A cold sweat broke out. She saw Jacob's mouth moving, but she couldn't concentrate on what he was saying. All she could think about was Andy suffering from a drug overdose. Her son! The one who wouldn't even take a painkiller when he sprained his ankle last year. She could name numerous occasions where he refused medication. Finally the feel of David's arm slipping around her pulled her back to the moment.

"We'll keep him here until I think he's out of danger," Jacob finished saying, then moved to her son's bed.

She started to follow, but David stopped her by tightening his arm about her shoulders.

"Lisa, how would Andy get the antidepressant? Do you take it?"

Her world tilted and spun before her eyes. She yanked away from him and faced him. "No." She dropped her voice to a fierce whisper. "And I don't make it a habit of leaving drugs around for my son or give them to him to take unless prescribed."

"I had to ask. If he didn't get it from you, then how did he get it? Remember Nancy saw him talking with Joey in the barn right before Emily found the same kind of medicine. There must be a connection."

"Yeah, Joey. He probably did something to my son."

"Maybe, but why?"

The doubt she saw flash into David's gaze—heard in his voice—hurt as much as angered her. "Because he doesn't like him. Have you forgotten the fight a few weeks ago?"

"No, I haven't. But what if Andy bought something from Joey? Have you considered that?"

"Yes, and that's not possible."

"Why?" His cop persona was fully in place.

"It just isn't," she muttered, her attention returning to her son lying in the hospital bed, pale, suddenly small in the midst of all the machines and equipment surrounding him. "Please leave. I can't be distracted at this moment." Her fury made her tremble at what David thought about her son.

David studied her for a few seconds, then seemed to decide something. His expression blank, he skirted around her and strode toward the door.

Jacob finished giving Andy the antidote and paused in front of her. "I heard what David said. Tell him about where Andy is coming from, about what you went through, your son went through. Make him understand what you and I know. Andy wouldn't be experimenting with drugs. At least not knowingly."

Lisa released her pent-up breath on a long sigh. "I will after I get my son home and I know he'll be all right. He's my focus now."

Jacob gave her a small smile. "I understand, but I need answers, too. Remember, drugs have come to the refuge. I can't have that."

"I'll do all I can. Andy isn't going to avoid my questions

after this." But how was she going to make him talk if he didn't want to? And how was she going to tell David about her past? Would he believe she was no longer connected with drugs?

Andy leaned into the railing as he climbed the stairs to the second-floor landing outside his apartment. Lisa watched him let himself into their place while she stood below with David, waiting for her son to disappear inside.

"I want to talk to you. Will you come up?" she finally asked, aware the hour was late but needing to have this conversation with the man she was all too aware was a police officer.

"Can this wait?"

Yes, forever. "No. Please, I wouldn't ask unless I thought it was important."

"Okay." He started up the steps.

"Do you want anything to drink?" she asked when she closed her front door.

"No."

"Let me check on Andy and make sure he's okay, then we can talk."

Without waiting for a reply, she strode down the short hall and went into her son's small bedroom. He lay in bed, the covers pulled up around his neck, his eyes closed. Brushing his hair back, she kissed him on the cheek and wondered if he was really asleep.

At the hospital before they'd left, she'd informed him about the antidepressants in his system, then told him that they needed to talk about what happened today. No more evasions. He'd nodded, started to say something, but at that moment David reappeared in the emergency room. Andy had clamped his lips together and peered away.

David had heard from Jacob that Andy could go home, and

David was there to drive them because he'd driven her to the hospital. Even with what happened today, she couldn't shut down her developing feelings toward David. He had been doing his job, and now she needed him to focus that on Joey—not Andy. Although she didn't relish saying anything to him about her past, she knew it was time and had accepted his offer of a ride.

Switching off the lamp on the table, Lisa tiptoed from Andy's bedroom, leaving the door ajar. Slowly she made her way back to the living room, fortifying herself with calming breaths the closer she came to David.

He stood before the window, the drapes not drawn yet, his hands jammed into his jeans pockets. When she entered, he pivoted toward her. A grim expression confronted her. He wasn't going to make it easy for her to confess her past sins.

"Have a seat." She waved her hand toward the chair across from the couch.

He closed the distance between them. "That's okay. I'm too wound up to sit."

"Okay." Then she would stand, too, although she was dead tired. "Earlier today you wanted to know why I'm sure Andy didn't purposely take an antidepressant and in this case more than a normal dosage." Although for a brief moment, she'd had her doubts, too, she didn't anymore. "I don't know how it ended up in Andy, but he didn't buy any from Joey and take it. He's a good kid."

"I've seen good kids turn to drugs."

"I didn't want to say anything to you at the hospital, but I want you to know about why I know Andy is innocent."

"Why now?"

"To make you understand what's going on with my son."

"Okay. What's going on?" David stepped back at the same time a barrier seemed to spring up between them.

She fixed her gaze on him. "Up until four years ago I was a drug addict whose habit landed my son in the foster care system. Seeing Andy stumbling around on the basketball court brought back all the horrors of being addicted to drugs— horrors my son was aware of." As she'd spoken the color bleached from David's face. Before she lost her nerve, she continued. "He won't even take an over-the-counter medication for a headache or his allergies. That's why I know he won't have anything to do with drugs. He knows what they can do to a person, how easily they can destroy a person's life because they nearly did mine."

"I see. Thanks for telling me." His voice came out in a monotone, no emotion revealed in his words or face.

Although the wall between her and David grew with her confession, her declaration had strengthened even more her belief her son was innocent of any wrongdoing at the refuge. For a while she'd forgotten how much of a struggle it had been for her and that Andy had been there every step of the way, giving her the motivation to succeed, loving her in spite of what she'd done.

"Tomorrow I'll be having a conversation with Andy. I'll get answers. This can't go on. His reaction to the antidepressant could have been fatal. Emily could have taken that pill today and…" She couldn't finish her statement. Tears clogged her throat.

An emotion—anger—glimmered in his eyes for a few seconds, then it was gone, masked by his neutral expression. "I need to go. Let me know what Andy says."

Cold. Impersonal. David was out the door before she'd moved a step. She went to the window that overlooked the parking lot, caught sight of him climbing into his Jeep and quickly pulled the drapes. Her hands quaked. Memories warred with her knowledge she'd done the right thing by telling him about her past.

The emotions she'd held at bay most of the day deluged her, suddenly and overpoweringly. Tears crowded her eyes, blurring her vision so much so that she had to feel her way to the chair. Collapsing into it, she buried her face in her hands and cried.

What if I'd lost Andy today from a drug overdose?

How am I going to deal with this?

Lord, help. I can't do this without You. You are my rock.

David rested his forehead against the steering wheel he gripped. Outside his Jeep, darkness ruled. But inside it reigned, too. A darkness of the soul. His hands clenched so tightly around the cold plastic that they locked in place. Although pain shot up his arms, he didn't care. He welcomed it. Maybe it would drive the past from his mind.

Everything came back to drugs. To people who became so addicted they would do anything for a score. It would never change. People didn't change.

Like Sodom and Gomorrah, popped into his thoughts.

He raised his head and looked up at Lisa's apartment. *Why, Lisa? I had begun to care about you. Were you once like that teenage girl I tried to protect and ended up killing a thirteen-year-old boy?*

Numb, drained of all feelings, David started his car. He had to get away from here. Put as much distance between himself and Lisa as possible.

He drove the streets of Cimarron City aimlessly, no place in mind. Saturday night. A bar's lighted sign mocked him as he passed it. He kept going. But for the first time in his life, he wanted to stop and drown himself in liquor as he'd seen some of his fellow police officers do to numb their emotions. He wouldn't go that route. He'd seen his share of good cops destroyed by alcohol. Somehow he would make it through the night.

* * *

"Ready, Max." David yelled from the bottom of the stairs at his sister's house.

The eight-year-old poked his head around the corner upstairs, his hair a mess, sticking straight up at odd angles. "Mom said I can't go to the game until I get my room cleaned."

David checked his watch. "I can wait fifteen minutes, then I've got to go."

Max grinned, said, "I'll get it done," then disappeared around the corner, the sound of pounding sneakers echoing through the house.

"What's going on?" Kelli asked from the entrance into the den.

"Your son has a deadline to get his room cleaned. I can't wait long."

Kelli spun on her heel. "Good. Come on in and let's talk."

Her tone announced he should race up the stairs and help his nephew clean instead of following her into the den. But that wouldn't stop her. He might as well get the conversation over with because she would pursue it. She could be so stubborn at times.

He entered the room but hung back at the entrance. "What's up?" he asked as if he didn't know what she wanted to talk about.

"Thanksgiving and the invitation you extended to Lisa and Andy." She whirled about, her hands on her waist. "She was coming and now she told me this morning she isn't. She didn't tell me why, but I have a feeling you know why."

"Yeah."

"Well, why?"

He came into the den a few feet and stopped, clutching the back of a lounge chair. "We haven't exactly spoken this week, but I have a feeling it has to do with what she told me last Saturday night."

"Did it have anything to do with what happened to Andy at the scrimmage game you had?"

"Yeah."

A long pause with his sister glaring at him. "Am I gonna have to drag the details out of you?"

"She told me some things about her past to help me understand why Andy couldn't have willingly taken the antidepressant found in his system."

"So?"

"I'm not at liberty to discuss the details."

"Why has she suddenly told me she and Andy aren't coming to dinner this Thursday?"

He averted his gaze and plowed his fingers through his hair. "She probably thinks I'm upset with her."

"Are you?"

"I don't know what I feel."

"Figure it out and fix it. She's a good friend who has been wonderful with the women at my shelter. There are some who've been on drugs, and with the setback in their situation have wanted to start using again—anything to take the pain away. She's the one who has helped them find another solution to their pain."

"She has?" She would know what those women were going through having been in that situation herself. *I've been wanting to change, anything to push the past away because what I'm doing isn't working. So, how has Lisa changed? Has she really? Or is it all some kind of pretense?*

"I'm planning on having her and Andy here Thursday, and you're going to make sure the invitation you issued is accepted. Don't come without them. Understood?"

He arched a brow. "Is there anything else you want?"

"Don't use that sarcastic tone with me." Kelli's mouth tightened into a frown. "Thanksgiving is meant to be shared. You had the right idea. We're gonna serve lunch at the shelter, then come back here for a small supper and celebrate the abundance the Lord has given us with family and friends."

"Yes, ma'am." He saluted his sister.

The sound of pounding sneakers filled the house as Max clamored down the stairs and raced into the room, skidding to a stop a few feet from David. Saved in the nick of time.

He walked with his nephew out to his Jeep. Right after the game, he would have to catch Lisa who had kept her distance all week when she'd picked up Andy from practice. He'd been fine with that because he thought that had been a good idea. But he had been concerned with the fact that Andy hadn't come to the third tae kwon do lesson this morning at the refuge. He needed to talk with Andy as well as his mother. But what was he supposed to say to a woman who had told him something from her past she wasn't proud of when he couldn't even face his own, let alone talk about it with another?

"We won, Mom!" Andy flung his arms around Lisa, then as though he remembered he was twelve and among his friends, dropped them and stepped back. But he didn't wipe the huge grin from his face.

"And you shot the winning basket. Way to go, hon."

After the players calmed down some, David waved them to him. "This was a tough game. You all did great. I'd like for us to go to The Ultimate Pizzeria for a little celebration. I'm treating."

That announcement met with a round of cheers from the boys, especially Andy who always felt at home at the restaurant. While David spoke with the parents and finalized the plans for the impromptu party, she stayed back. She would have let Andy go with one of his friends, but with it being at The Ultimate Pizzeria, she couldn't very well not go. She would keep her distance though from David. He had made it clear he didn't want to have anything to do with her.

Last Sunday he'd called but immediately asked to speak with Andy. Her son had talked for a few minutes, assuring his coach he was doing all right. That had been the only contact she'd really had with David since her confession. What else did she expect from a police officer who had seen enough drug addicts in his profession not to want to have anything to do with one—even a recovering addict?

While Andy slipped on his sweatpants and jacket, she gathered her purse and started for the door. David loped toward her and caught up with her near the entrance into the gym. He pulled her to the side so people could leave.

"You're coming to the party, aren't you?" His hand still cupped her elbow.

The touch quickened her heartbeat. She tapped down her automatic reaction to him. She didn't want to care about the man. She didn't need to open herself up to heartache. The past week had dragged with endless nights. Lying awake in bed rehashing the whole weekend before, wanting David to tell her everything would be okay. She wanted her jogging partner back.

"Because it's at The Ultimate Pizzeria, it wouldn't look good if I'm not there. I'll even cut you a deal." She tugged away from him.

"Good. I want to tell you about what I've learned so far—" he leaned close so no one could hear him "—about what happened last weekend."

"Obviously you didn't find anything to connect Joey to what he did to Andy or he wouldn't be on the team." Disappointment toughened her voice to a raw whisper.

"Not yet. But I do have something." He stepped to the side

to allow her to leave because Andy was approaching her. "See you in a little while."

What do you have? She wanted to shout that question at David's retreating back, but she didn't. The second she got a chance at The Ultimate Pizzeria, however, she would ask that very thing, then put the restaurant between them because when she was near him she began to have hope for more, and his silence made it clear there wasn't more.

Chapter Seven

"Mom, I'm gonna go play some video games. Okay?" Andy hopped up from his seat.

"Sure."

Lisa watched him race away with several other teammates and wished he had stayed. When she had arrived at the restaurant, after she'd checked to make sure everything was running smoothly, she'd told Nathan who was working the cash register to give any team member and their family her discount. Then she'd placed her order and snagged herself and Andy a table for two. By the time David had entered and put in what he wanted to eat, she'd been safely seated. She'd needed time to regroup. If only she could erase her past.

The second Andy disappeared into the game room, David slipped into the chair her son had vacated. "I didn't realize how busy tonight would be. I won't be able to stay long. I should help out in the back since I'm here." His presence so close she could reach across the table and touch him—wanted to badly— brought all the self-berating this past week to the foreground. How different her life would have been if she'd never taken that first drug so long ago. Maybe then she would have had a chance at a normal life—with a man to love.

"Why did you tell me about your drug problem?"

His question threw her off kilter. "I—" she swallowed hard, "—I didn't want any secrets between us. And I don't have a problem now."

"Your drug problem was a secret?" Again little emotion appeared on his face—all except a tic in his jaw as if he were clenching his teeth.

"Well, not exactly. I certainly don't go around advertising my past, but everyone connected with the refuge knows about it. They are the ones who helped me through it. Them and the Lord."

Both of his eyebrows rose. "The Lord?"

"Yes, I went to a shelter connected with my church. Of course, at the time it wasn't my church. Knowing the Lord was with me every step of the way helped me through some tough times when I wanted to slip back into old patterns."

"You don't anymore?"

Skepticism edged his question, and her heart bled at the sound. *Lord, what do I say to this man to make him understand I'm not the same person I was four years ago?* All she could be was honest. "A year ago I might have said yes, but no. There's no appeal for me. *None.* I've seen too many whose lives were destroyed because of drugs. Some of those were women I tried to help at the shelter your sister runs. They ended up going back to the same abusive situation. They didn't have the support I did, or they didn't want anyone to help them."

"Are you talking about God or the people at the refuge?"

"Both, but mostly God. In the middle of the night He was the one I turned to when I was hurting and wanting a fix. He held me in His arms and wouldn't let go."

David frowned. "So you've changed?"

His cynicism cut deep, opening healed wounds. For so many years she had never felt she was worthy of love or anything good and lasting. Then she found the Lord's love and knew that wasn't the case. She wasn't going to let this man take her back to that place. In fact, she was going to fight to change his mind. The second she thought that she wanted to snatch it back because that would mean she'd have to be around him to do that and that would only cause her more pain. *Haven't I had my quota yet? Lord, how much do I have to hurt before enough is enough?*

But no matter how much she tried to deny what God wanted her to do, she couldn't. *Okay, Lord, I'm in until the end whatever that may be. But I'm gonna need Your guidance.*

Calmness descended, and she relaxed again. "Yes, I have. If you have the courage, get to know me and you'll see."

"Because you're being *honest* with me, I'll be honest with you. Your revelation has thrown me, to say the least. I thought we had something going with us, but to find out I didn't really know you at all really makes me wary." He kept his expression neutral, his voice void of emotions.

"But the person I've been with you is me." She tapped her chest. "This is me now. The person I told you about doesn't exist anymore. Haven't you done something you're regretted and wished you could do over?"

He flinched. Something flickered in his gaze but dissipated before she could read it. "Everyone has regrets, I'm sure." He looked away for a long moment, then back into her eyes. "We're gonna serve Thanksgiving dinner at the shelter, then have something at Kelli's house later in the evening. She wants you and Andy to come for Thanksgiving. Will you reconsider?

But not you. His unsaid words pierced through the wall she was desperately trying to erect around her heart to protect herself from further pain. "Yes, we will," she murmured, her mouth dry while her throat burned with unshed tears she wouldn't dare release in front of him. *He wants nothing to do with me. He is gonna hurt me. You are asking too much.*

"Great, Kelli will be pleased." He started to rise.

"What have you found out about Joey?" Lisa asked before he left.

He paused and sat again, folding his arms on the table and scanning the area around them. "I talked with the principal at the middle school and found out she thinks there's a ring of students selling prescription drugs, but she doesn't know who or have any concrete evidence. They have done surprise searches, but haven't found any drugs on anyone."

"What did she say about Joey? Did she think he could be involved?"

"He's on a list of suspects she's keeping an eye on. As I am at ball practice. Also Roman had a talk with Ryan, and the boy said nothing happened, that Joey and his friends just wanted to know about various kids at the refuge. I'm assuming Andy didn't say anything because you didn't say."

"All I know is my son promised me he had nothing to do with taking drugs. He doesn't know how he ended up taking an antidepressant. And he reemphasized Joey is bad news."

"Someone could have slipped it into a drink. It's tasteless and colorless. It takes a while to have an effect so it was probably right before he started playing the game. He said he had a sports drink beforehand. That's probably how. What were he and Joey arguing about in the barn?"

At least David sounded at if he now believed Andy didn't intentionally take the drug. Thankfully revealing her past had caused him to rethink the conclusion he'd come to concerning her son. "He told Joey to leave his friends alone, that if he finds out he's trying to sell them anything he would tell, that Joey wouldn't catch him off guard again like after practice. Then Andy grabbed Ryan and pulled him away from the group of boys."

David leaned forward, his lime-scented aftershave wafting to Lisa. "So Andy suspects something?"

"He's heard a few rumblings but really nothing else. Joey has always schemed to make money, according to my son." Lisa took a drink of her ice water, his nearness causing her pulse to speed. When would his presence not affect her? She needed to get to that place soon.

"What's Joey's brother like?"

"He's a good worker. Always on time. Does what he's asked. And although he dropped out last spring, he's been going to school this year to finish up."

"He's had a few brushes with the law. Some of his friends who dropped out of school have gone on to do some time."

"Maybe Mitch is trying to change."

"Maybe."

"I like to believe the best until proven otherwise."

He grinned. "And I'm the opposite."

"Have you always felt that way?"

David shook his head. "There was a time I believed as you."

"What happened?" If she were going to help him, she needed to get to know him, not just how he was now but also in the past.

He lifted one shoulder. "My job. One of the hazards of being a cop."

"Hazards? That's an interesting way to put it. It makes you sound like you regret being that way."

"There's something to being an innocent."

"Because you know my background, you know I haven't been that way in a long time."

"And yet you have that Pollyanna outlook."

"Yes, I believe in hope. I'm living proof people do change if they have a good reason to."

"You mean Andy—" David started, but Andy rushed up to the table and interrupted him.

"Mom, there's a problem in the game room." Concern, mixed with urgency, vibrated from her son.

"What's wrong?" Lisa asked, rising.

"I saw Joey give another kid something. That kid gave Joey some money in return. Then Joey headed toward the restroom after another boy from school went in. I started to follow Joey when his brother, Mitch, went into there, too. I think Joey has drugs on him and he's gonna make another exchange."

David surged to his feet. "I'll take care of this."

He strode toward the men's room. Lisa and Andy hurried after David. Would this be the break they were looking for? Lisa hoped so, but she hated to see Mitch involved. He was a good employee, and she preferred to think he was trying to make his life better as she had. He'd told her that once when they had been closing up together. She wanted to believe he wasn't lying.

Halfway across the open restaurant David spied a young boy slip out of the restroom, fear on his face. David hurried his pace, memorizing the child's face so he could find him later.

At the door he turned toward Lisa and Andy who were right behind him. "You both stay outside and make sure no one else comes in."

David pushed the door open a few inches and reached toward his gun in his holster. But his hand shook so badly he didn't think he could hold it. Sweat beaded his forehead. Joey was thirteen years old, just like the kid he'd killed because of a drug deal going down.

Lord, if You're listening, please don't let there be a repeat.

He continued inside the restroom without pulling his weapon.

It might be a stupid move, but he couldn't pass up the chance to catch Joey red-handed and possibly put an end to what he was doing. Easing through the doorway, he moved quietly toward the voices he heard around the corner.

"Give them to me. You aren't going to deal. You won't make the same mistakes I did. You have a chance to make something of yourself."

Unless there was more than Joey and his older brother in here, Mitch must have said that because of the deeper pitch. David inched closer until he could get a glimpse of what was going on in the room by the teens' reflections in the mirror mounted on the wall over the sinks.

"Leave me alone. This isn't your business." Joey stood with his hands straight at his sides, his fingers clutching a plastic baggie with a lot of different pills in it. "Since when do you care what I do? You're always too busy for me."

"I'm trying to support us. That takes money."

Joey shook the bag of drugs in his brother's face. "This is money. Easy money."

"Dad's gone. It's just you and me now." Mitch pushed his brother's hand away from him. "It's wrong. I've seen my friends all go to jail because of drugs. I'm not gonna see you end up there, too."

David took a deep breath and turned the corner. "And neither am I."

Joey's eyes widened. Then suddenly he whirled and slammed open a stall door. David surged forward, but Mitch beat him to Joey. He yanked his little brother back into the main room and wrenched the baggie from his grip.

Mitch's gaze lit upon the holster clipped on David's belt under his jacket. "You a cop?"

"Yup."

Mitch thrust his little brother behind him. "These were mine." He held the assortment of pills, jiggling them in the baggie. "He was trying to stop me from using them."

"Son, I heard enough to know that's not true. You were trying to stop him from selling these." David took the plastic bag from Mitch. "So quit trying to protect him. He needs help."

"Help?" Mitch snarled. "No one offered me any. I had to do it all on my own."

"Well, Joey's got me." David said as he flipped open his cell to call the police station. Amazed by what he'd said, he thought about taking back his declaration. But he couldn't. Maybe this was what he was supposed to do. He wasn't sure anymore. Something was missing from his life.

The Wednesday before Thanksgiving, David climbed from his Jeep, several squad cars parked in the lot next to The Ultimate Pizzeria. Quickly striding toward the entrance, he tamped down his worry and concern, trying to wear his professional facade while in reality all he wanted to do was burst through the doors and scoop Lisa into his arms to make sure she wasn't harmed in any way. When the robbery had been reported, there hadn't been a mention of anyone being hurt. But what if Lisa was? He could have made it to the restaurant before an ambulance, having broken a few speeding laws on his way to the crime.

Inside the pizzeria he surveyed the scene before him. The uniforms had the witnesses cordoned off in one room to the left. One police officer stood at the entrance and nodded toward him when he entered the place.

On his way to the two cops standing by the cash register, David veered toward the room where about a dozen witnesses were and peered in. Where was Lisa? Drawing in a fortifying breath, he continued his trek toward the officers at the counter. Maybe she wasn't at work when the robbery went down.

Behind David his partner came into the restaurant and hurried to catch up with him.

"What fire was lit under your tail?" he asked David. "The robbery had already gone down. You'd think you were trying to race here to stop it."

David glanced at the older man. "I know someone who works here."

"Is she here?"

"She?"

"Yes, from the look on your face it has to be a woman who has you all concerned."

"Don't know if she is, I just got here."

His partner took out his pad and pen. "I'll take care of this. You start interviewing the witnesses."

At the counter David asked the officer nearest him, "Where's the manager on duty?"

The cop jerked his thumb toward the back. "She's retrieving the surveillance footage for us. Tim is back there with her. All the cameras feed into a computer in her office."

David strode through the kitchen. She was okay. His breathing returned to normal until he stood in the doorway and saw Lisa giving the evidence to the police officer, her hands shaking so badly she nearly dropped a CD. An ashen cast to her skin heightened her huge blue eyes and the look of fear in them.

"That covers the last hour."

Her quavering voice penetrated the hard shell he'd cocooned his emotions concerning Lisa in.

"Thank you, ma'am," Tim said, his attention resting on David at the same time Lisa's swept to him.

"I'll take it from here, officer. Give that tape to my partner out in the main room."

When the man left, Lisa crumbled into her chair at her desk, her arms hanging listlessly. In her lap she laced her fingers together to tightly the knuckles whitened. The urge to hold her inundated him. He stayed in the entrance into the office, fighting the need, remembering all that had happened in the past ten days. An eternity to him. He'd missed her laughter, smile and yet how could they pick up where they had left off before her confession?

The pounding of his heartbeat in his ears mimicked the ticking of a clock as time passed, neither of them saying a word, making a move.

Finally she lifted her gaze to his. "Do you have any questions for me?"

The crack in her voice at the end of the question further opened the rift in his protective shell. He took a step toward her and opened his mouth, but no words would come.

"I was at the counter when the—three masked men—came into…" Her voice ground to halt. She swallowed several times. "Into the rest…"

Tears brimmed in her eyes and his emotions poured out of the fissure. He knelt by her and took her hand. "I'm so sorry, Lisa."

"One waved a gun in my face. Had me back away from the cash register while the other stuffed the bag with the money. I tried to tell him we didn't have much money. The one with the gun just shouted at me to shut up. I thought…" The rush of her words stopped as tears flowed down her cheeks. "I thought he was going to shoot me."

David pulled her to her feet and sheltered her against him. "Shh. You don't have to say anything. I can get your statement later."

The sound of her anguish made him feel so helpless. He stroked her back and cradled her as though she would break at any moment. Somehow he would catch this robbery gang.

"Why is Joey here?" Andy asked Lisa when they entered the women's shelter.

"To help serve Thanksgiving dinner like us."

"But he's in trouble. He broke the law."

Lisa stepped away from the entrance and to the side so no one would hear their conversation. "Andy, David told me he was bringing Joey to help here and then have dinner with us at Kelli's. Mitch will be here, too. Joey will have to face his crime through the juvenile system. He isn't getting off scot-free."

"But—but Joey's probably the one who slipped me the drug. He'll probably try something here."

"David's trying to help him."

"Why?"

"Because it's the right thing to do. We should try and help, too."

His lips puckered into a pout. "I don't like this."

"Maybe Joey needs the right friend to show him the way."

"Well, that's not gonna be me," Andy muttered while walking away.

Lisa started to follow her son across the dining room toward the kitchen when Mitch entered. She stopped to speak to her employee. "Are you okay after the robbery yesterday?"

"Yeah. Having a gun waved in your face can make a person definitely look at his life. How about you?"

"All I wanted to do was hold Andy last night." *And be held by David again.* "I'm glad you could make it, Mitch."

"I wanted to be with my brother for Thanksgiving, and this was the only way. I'm all he has now."

"How long has your father been gone?"

"A few months. I'm nineteen, but I don't think the court is gonna let me be Joey's guardian after what happened."

After David took Joey to the police station, the state stepped in. Joey had spent the first few days in juvenile detention until a judge made a tentative ruling to be reviewed later. The state had custody of him now, and he had been sent to Stone's Refuge. "For the time being he's in a good place. The fifth cottage at the refuge is for boys who need more guidance. Thankfully there was a place for Joey."

"Yeah, but he ain't too happy."

"I didn't think he would be. He needs help, but he doesn't see it that way."

Mitch looked toward his younger brother. "When I called him last night, he spent most of the time complaining about the program he has to complete before the court will even consider who'll be his guardian."

"It's based on a relationship-healing model. I've heard good things about the Seven Steps to Healing."

"I don't know how much he'll cooperate."

Lisa began walking toward the kitchen area with Mitch next to her. "If he wants things to change, he'll need to."

"He's hardheaded." Mitch shook his head. "The house parent had him mucking out the horses' stalls yesterday afternoon because he started a fight and was put in detention at school. I was like Joey. I know it doesn't get you anyplace, all that anger lashing out, but he doesn't."

"And he's not listening to you either?"

"No. He doesn't understand why I'm working so hard and not making much money. I told him until I graduate from high school I'm limited in what I can do—legally. I'm finishing up high school this semester. I have plans to go on to college—someday."

"Good for you." Lisa stepped into the large kitchen. "Be patient. I'm sure it will work out in the end."

"I'll try. What should I do here today?" Mitch asked, scanning the people all busy at various stations.

"I just got here and I haven't asked. Let's find Kelli. She runs the shelter."

Kelli stood in front of a counter with the cabinet open, removing dinner plates from the shelf. After forming several stacks, she sidled to another cupboard and took down glasses.

"Kelli, this is Mitch, Joey's brother. We both want to know how we can help."

"Mitch, how about you grab Joey, Andy and Abbey and get them to set the tables? My daughter is around here somewhere." Kelli peered around the teenager. "Ah, there's Abbey. I was afraid she'd skipped out." She gestured toward her daughter across the room, lounging against the wall, arms folded over her chest.

After Mitch left to gather his helpers, Lisa asked, "How about me?"

"Help my brother decorate the pumpkin cupcakes. I've got all you'll need set up at the table over there. Your main job will be to keep David from eating any. Tell him I have a pumpkin cheesecake at home for later tonight. That ought to satisfy him for the time being." Kelli waved her hand toward the area. "Most everything else is almost done. David just finished carving the turkeys. I've just finished whipping up the mashed potatoes. All I have to do is take the bean casseroles and dressing out of the ovens and we'll be ready."

"Isn't there anything else I can do?" Lisa glanced at the table off to the side that Kelli indicated. Two chairs sat side by side—only a foot apart. She'd seen David less than twenty-four hours ago at the robbery scene at The Ultimate Pizzeria. That whole few hours was a blur to her, even when he'd insisted on taking her home and making sure Hannah came to stay with her. But the one thing she did remember was the feel of his arms about her. For a short while she'd felt secured and comforted. But now this was reality—one where her past still hung between them.

"I thought you and David had settled your differences."

"We're working on it."

Kelli leaned close and whispered, "When it comes to my brother I've decided he's clueless about women."

"It's complicated." *As my life has been lately.*

Lisa approached the workplace and took a chair, scooting it to the end, several feet away from where David would sit. She could still remember smelling his lime-scented aftershave the other night and how her pulse quickened. How he had comforted her after the robbers. She was falling in love and saw no future with David. With the other aromas, pumpkin, dressing, turkey, spicing the air, she should be safe, but just in case, this three-foot separation should take care of it.

In front of her were about four dozen cupcakes and a large bowl of butter cream frosting. In a smaller one there were candy corns to place on top of the iced desserts. As she picked up a knife, David emerged from a walk-in refrigerator to her left side and took his seat.

"How are you doing, Lisa? Did you get any sleep last night?"

She connected with his serious look. "Better today than yesterday, but no sleep."

"I can imagine. I'm going to get that robbery gang. They've become bolder. They'll make a mistake and I'll be there to get them."

The vehement tone in his voice convinced Lisa if anyone could, it would be David. She could still feel and remember his arms about her while he whispered words of comfort. For that brief time he'd held her she'd felt totally safe. His solace the day before had made her yearn for more, but after what had happened when she told him about her past, she didn't think that was possible.

"Thanks for coming." He grinned, a dimple in his cheek appearing. "I'd have been in hot water with my sister if you hadn't. And frankly, I have enough to deal with with Joey. I think I've bit off more than I can handle."

"I was surprised by that."

"So was I. I picked Joey up at the refuge to spend the day with us, and the whole way he glared out the windshield, not saying one word. I understand he asked Roman when he would get out of 'prison,' which is his word for the refuge." David iced one cupcake, then picked up another.

"He's lucky he got into the drug program at the refuge and didn't go to juvenile detention. The only reason he isn't is you pulled a few strings and know Peter and Roman. Maybe you should give him an idea of what a real prison is like. If he continues on the path he's been taking, that's where he'll end up. That or dead."

"That's a wonderful idea! That's what I'm gonna do. I even know a group he can visit to hear from prisoners about what goes on inside."

"Why did you take Joey on? Andy was so upset when he heard he was going to be here. I had to threaten him with grounding if he didn't come."

"I'm sorry. I'll talk with Andy. And as for the reason, I'm not sure I can put it into words." David scooped some more frosting onto his butter knife and lathered another cupcake with it. "Something's lacking in my life. I guess you could say I'm searching."

"I used to feel that way."

"Used to? What changed for you?"

"I found a purpose. If you don't have a purpose, you just go through the motions of living."

"What's your purpose?"

"To live a life in Christ, which means staying off drugs."

"So your faith has stopped you from relapsing?"

She nodded, finishing her thirteenth cupcake. "That and not letting Andy down like that ever again."

"You make it sound easy, but I've dealt with enough addicts to know it isn't."

"And you're right. I didn't come to this place in my life easily. I did have a relapse in my first few months in rehab, and I ended up in the hospital. My ex-boyfriend beat me up, and if Hannah and Jacob hadn't found me, no telling if I'd have been here right now. It was snowing and I was in an alley, going in and out of consciousness. I could have frozen to death if they hadn't come when they did on Christmas Eve."

"You think bringing Joey to church will help?"

"It won't hurt. I'll pray that he'll be open to hearing what the Lord says. But truthfully he might have to hit rock bottom before he's ready to listen to anyone."

"You hit rock bottom?" His gaze captured hers, genuine interest in the depth of his eyes.

That look sparked hope in Lisa. "Yes. I'd lost my son and knew I couldn't stay with my boyfriend. I didn't have a job and no means of support. Hannah and Jacob got me into a homeless shelter run by their church. They gave me hope."

David looked at her long and hard. Before he could say anything, though, shouting from the dining room warned Lisa of trouble brewing with Andy yelling at Joey. She pushed to her feet and hurried toward the sound. She heard David's chair scraping across the tile behind her.

"You can't do anything right! That's not how to set a table." Andy stood nose-to-nose with Joey, both boys' hands fisted at their sides.

"Who in the world wants to set a table anyway?" Joey thrust out his chest, almost bumping into Andy.

Lisa was halfway across the room when Mitch stepped in between the boys. "I do for my job. Here let me show you." The older teen moved to the nearest table and started putting out the dishes.

Joey snorted and spun around, fleeing the room.

David sighed next to her. "I'd better make sure he doesn't run away. Can you finish the cupcakes?"

"Yes. Go. I need to speak with Andy."

As David left the dining room, Lisa faced her son whose features had hardened into a fierce frown. "Andy, are you all right?" It wasn't like her son not to be patient, caring of others. He often taught the younger kids at the refuge various jobs.

"He doesn't belong here. He needs to be…" His anger choked off his words, his cheeks flushed cherry red.

"You need to work on forgiving Joey. He needs your help, hon. He's in a lot of pain, but he won't admit that. His father left him and Mitch. He has trouble in school. According to you, not many friends, and the ones he has aren't good for him. He needs a friend like you." The second she said it she wished she could take it back because she wasn't sure she really wanted Andy and Joey to be friends. Forgiving was one thing, but befriending was another.

His eyes huge, Andy worked his mouth but nothing came out.

"I didn't say forgiving Joey would be easy, just something you need to think about doing. I've done a lot of things wrong in my life, and thankfully the Lord forgave me, no questions asked. He expects the same from us." As she spoke, she realized that even if David never forgave her, the Lord had. It was time she forgave herself.

"I don't know that I can, Mom."

She started to draw him into a hug, but her son shrugged away.

"I've got work to do, especially because Joey left." Andy evaded her and took his dishes and utensils to a table at the other end of the room.

Lord, give me the patience to show Andy the way.

David found Joey outside on the street, his hands rammed into his pockets, hunkered against the side of the building. The wind whipped down the street, stirring the fallen leaves in a swirl. The chill bit right through David. Like Joey he hadn't retrieved his coat before leaving the shelter.

Joey took one look at David and pivoted away, but the teen went only a few feet. "I ain't talking."

"Then listen. You have a choice here. You can either go through the program at the refuge or go to the juvenile detention center. If you think the refuge is a prison, then remember what the detention center was like."

"Yeah, right. I can't do a thing. What can be worse? I have to go through some stupid program about building good relationships. Ain't nothing wrong with my life. I get along just fine with the people I want to."

"The way you're heading your life will end one of two ways—dying young or ending up in prison."

Joey straightened to his full height, but in the process shivered from the piercing cold, defeating the purpose of the defiant gesture. "We'll all die one day."

"We can talk inside."

Joey raised his chin a notch. "What's the matter? Is a little cold too much for ya?"

"Then we'll talk out here. Why were you on the basketball team?"

Joey batted his eyes rapidly, as though he were surprised by the question, before he managed to mask his expression behind a stoic facade. He shrugged. "You tell me."

"I think you like to play the game. You're good at it when you keep your mind on it."

He glared at David. "You took care of that. I'm off the team. Remember?"

The hostility flowed off the teen, striking David. In his profession he'd dealt with these kinds of intense emotions often, but this was personal and he wasn't going to let this child push him away. He'd committed himself to helping Joey—somehow. "You're welcome back when you apologize to your teammates and have given up drugs—selling and taking."

"Yeah, well, don't hold your breath. I don't need y'all." Joey folded his arms across his chest and tried to cover up a shudder.

But I need you. That thought came unbidden into David's mind and stunned him. Was Joey his purpose? Was helping Joey going to heal him? He didn't have answers, just knew he had to do this.

"I used to think I didn't need anyone either. Life gets awfully lonely without people in it."

"I have friends. I just don't need you and the others on the team."

One of his so-called friends when questioned gave him up for spiking Andy's sports drink. David intended to show Joey the difference between a good and a bad friend. First, he was going to take Joey to church Sunday. Second, he was going to give him a tour of a prison and then a part of town where druggies hung out. He wanted Joey to see what became of people on drugs after a while.

"That's your choice. We're there for you if you change your mind, though."

Joey tossed his head toward the shelter's entrance. "Yeah, that looked like Andy was on my side in there."

"Do you blame him? You doctored his drink with an anti-depressant."

"I was doing him a favor. Showing him what a good time he could have. He's such a nerd."

"At least now you aren't denying you did it." A strong gust pierced any warmth David had managed to generate.

Joey's shoulders hunched forward, his teeth chattering. "What good would that do? Sam said I did it, and y'all believed him."

"Are you telling me you didn't?"

"Would you believe me if I did?"

"Depends."

Joey stared at David for a long moment.

The front door opened, the sound drawing David's gaze away. Lisa exited the shelter, his coat in her hand along with Joey's. Seeing her lifted David's spirits like a ray of light penetrating the darkness.

"I thought you two could use these." She handed him his, then gave Joey his jacket.

The child snatched it and quickly donned it while David slipped into his. In the short time he had been outside he hadn't realized how cold he'd become until the warmth encased him. But when he glanced back at Joey, the teen still shivered.

"We need to serve the ladies and their children soon. Are you two coming in to help?" Lisa asked, concern in her eyes when she looked at Joey, obviously chilled, his face pasty white with a tinge of blue on his lips. "We need you two." She directed the last sentence at Joey.

"Oh, I guess I can help." The teen pushed between them and hurried toward the door.

"Thank you. I wasn't sure if I could get him back inside. You gave him an out."

"Glad to help. I'm gathering your conversation didn't go well."

"Nope, but I didn't expect Joey to all of a sudden become my new best bud."

She chuckled, lightening the serious mood. "Let's go in. Maybe helping others will end up helping him."

"Anything is possible."

"Yes, there's always hope."

Hope. He'd lost that a long time ago. Was that what he needed? Hope that he would get his life back together. Hope that he would wake up each day and have a reason to drive his life. Hope that people could really change.

Chapter Eight

Sitting in Kelli's den, sated after a wonderful Thanksgiving meal, Lisa cupped her mug of hot chocolate and listened as each person told what they were thankful for. Joey had refused to say anything while Andy across the room from his ex-teammate had announced he was thankful for not being hurt by the antidepressant given to him the previous weekend. Both boys glared at each other. The silence in the room had grown until David coughed and asked if anyone wanted refills on their drink.

Finally her turn came. Lisa placed her mug on the coaster on the coffee table in front of the couch where she sat with David next to her. All gazes, accept Joey's, were fastened on her. Having come to a decision a moment before, she squared her shoulders and leaned forward. "I'm thankful for the Lord's love and mercy. I'm thankful for sitting here with you, drug-free with a plan for my life."

"Drug-free?" Kelli asked in a chair next to the roaring fire.

Lisa glanced down at her hands now clasped together tightly. Her courage wavered. She sucked in a deep breath and plunged ahead. "Yes. Four years ago at this time I was struggling to get off drugs and not doing a good job. My son was taken away from me. Although I wanted to keep my focus on getting Andy back and becoming clean, I kept thinking about my next fix. Then one snowy night I nearly died and knew I couldn't keep going with what I was doing or I would end up in the morgue. The Lord took me under His wing, and I'm proud to say I'm drug-free and have been for almost four years."

"I didn't know." Kelli's gaze strayed toward her brother for a few seconds, then returned to Lisa. "Thank you for sharing. No wonder you're so good with some of the ladies at the shelter. You've walked in their shoes."

"And never want to again." Lisa scanned the faces of the people in the room, finally stopping at Joey. He'd raised his head and looked right at her. For just a moment she saw puzzlement in his eyes before he peered at the floor near his feet.

Silence reigned, the crackling of the fire the only sound.

David slipped his hand over hers. She peered at him. Admiration shone in his blue depths, sending a warmth through her that rivaled the blaze in the grate.

He leaned toward her and whispered into her ear, "That took courage. Thanks for trying to help Joey."

She gave him a smile. "Your turn."

"I'm thankful for coming to Cimarron City, being with my family and—" he squeezed her clasped hands "—friends."

After a few seconds when David didn't continue, Max popped forward on the other side of his uncle. "I'm thankful Christmas is almost here."

"Max!"

"Well, I am, Mom. I've been waiting all year."

David's chuckle drew Lisa's attention to his face, relaxed, all the tension that had come and gone throughout the day with Joey melted away. He angled toward her and caught her staring at him. A flush warmed her cheeks. She looked down. For a few seconds she'd felt special in his eyes, as though she were important to him, as if he didn't know about her past. But he did. She sobered, trying to squelch her feelings toward David.

"Now that everyone has finished, I need someone to help me do the dishes." David rose. "I told Kelli I would clean up if she would cook. Any volunteers?" His penetrating gaze implored her to accept.

The kids all glanced away from David.

Unable to deny his silent request, Lisa stood next to David. "I will. After that delicious meal, I'd be glad to."

As she left the den trailing David, she heard Max ask if anyone wanted to play charades. There were a few groans, but Mitch jumped in and started organizing everyone into two teams.

"Maybe I'd better stay," Lisa said out in the hallway. "Mitch has Andy and Joey on the same team. That's not a good idea."

"Let's see what happens. Joey probably won't participate anyway. We're only a room away if there's any trouble."

"I guess nothing will happen with Kelli in there."

David pushed open the door into the kitchen. "Which do you want to do, wash or dry?"

"Wash. I wouldn't want you to get dishpan hands."

He laughed. "My hands are like leather whereas yours aren't. Let me wash. You dry what doesn't go into the dishwasher."

"You won't get an argument from me."

"Oh, I've got to remember that. Thanks for helping me. I was hoping you would."

"You did?"

Starting with the stack of dirty plates, he rinsed each one, then passed it to Lisa. "Yeah, I wanted to ask you about the Sunday school classes. Is there one you think would help Joey?"

"You could have asked your sister. She goes to the same church."

"I know, but she would make a big deal out of me attending. I'm trying to postpone that as long as possible."

"You've been away from church a long time?"

"Since my first year on the force," David answered, giving her the last plate, then starting on the glasses.

"Because of what you saw as a cop?"

"Yeah, it's kinda hard to think there's a God who cares when such horrible things happen."

"Then why do you think this will help Joey?"

He stopped and turned toward her. "You said the Lord helped you quit, so maybe the same could happen for Joey."

But not for him. David had all but said that. "I'm not so sure he's in the same place as I was."

He resumed rinsing the rest of the dishes. "Okay, chalk it up to desperation. I don't know what to do to help him, but I'm gonna help him somehow."

"Why are you so intent on helping him?"

"I have to."

"Why?"

He tensed.

Even from his profile, Lisa could see a war being waged within David. She expected him to dismiss her question, but he released a long sigh and turned off the water, then pivoted toward her, only a foot between.

"Because I killed the thirteen-year-old brother of a drug dealer. He was shooting at me and a teenage drug user. I didn't know it was just a kid when I returned fire, but I haven't been able to get the child's face out of my mind."

"When did this happen?" she asked, shocked that he would tell her something like this.

"Almost two years ago in Dallas. I've been haunted ever since. I've never killed a person before. I'd…" His voice thickened and he bent forward, gripping the edge of the counter. "Worse, in the confusion of the exchange, the drug dealer brother escaped. We never caught him, and he's out there I'm sure, corrupting others. The whole bust was for nothing."

"He knew his brother was there?"

"I'm sure he did."

A coldness bore into her heart. "And he didn't care."

"No, but even knowing he used his own little brother as a lookout/enforcer hasn't made me forget what I'd done."

Clasping his arm, she spun him toward her. "What did you do? You protected yourself and the teenager. What else were you supposed to do? Let the boy shoot you, possibly her." Ten years ago she could have been that girl. Now she totally understood David's emotions tangled up in her confession of the past. And she couldn't blame him. In his eyes, he'd always look at her with that incident in Dallas in mind. But she could help him. The Lord saved her. He could do the same for David, and she could show him the way.

"I've told myself all that." Pain glazed his eyes. "I—I…" He swallowed hard. "That doesn't erase the fact I killed someone."

"But when you became a police officer, you knew that was a possibility."

"Yeah, but knowing is one thing. Actually doing it is entirely different."

"So you've been having a pity party for the past two years?"

"Whoa. You don't pull any punches."

"Helping Joey won't change the past. Won't bring the kid you killed back to life. I'm not saying you shouldn't help Joey, but it won't make it better. It won't change the facts."

He twisted away from her, pulling his arm from her grasp.

"But it could make up for taking a life." He moved to the stove and grabbed the pans still sitting there.

"It doesn't work that way."

He rounded on her. "What way?"

"Guilt won't go away because you do a good deed. It'll still be there waiting to come out when you least expect it."

"So you're saying for the rest of my life I'm gonna feel guilty over this kid's death."

"Maybe. But you might think about asking the Lord for help. He was there for me. He can be there for you."

David turned away and gathered up all the pans, then brought them to the sink. "Is Andy coming to the tae kwon do class this Saturday?"

"With Joey off the team, there shouldn't be any more problems."

"I still think he can benefit from learning it, but it's your call. I personally would like him to come. I want to get to know him better. Your son's influence is what a child like Joey needs."

"Andy doesn't want to have anything to do with Joey. You saw what happened today at the shelter."

"And I don't think Joey wants to have anything to do with Andy, but that doesn't change the fact that Andy would be a good role model for him." David squirted soap into the sink and then turned on the hot water.

Andy and Joey together. She couldn't see it. "I don't know if I want Andy hanging out with someone like Joey." Earlier she'd encouraged her son to help Joey, but that didn't mean she wanted him to get close to the kid. She wanted to do the right thing, but the protective mother in her kept interfering with what she knew the Lord would want.

"You've given your son some good values to live by. Trust he will do the right thing."

"Trust him? You're telling me to and you don't trust anyone." *Especially me.* That thought cut her to the core. "There was a time you didn't trust Andy, either." Her throat closed around the last sentence.

He swung his gaze to hers, an intensity in his expression that stole her breath. "I trusted you when I told you about the thirteen-year-old I killed. My sister doesn't even know."

His declaration stunned Lisa and robbed her of any reply. He'd given her a rare gift. The significance of it overwhelmed her. "Why did you?" she finally asked when she didn't think her voice would crack. "Especially in light of my past."

"Because you shared a part of yourself with me and then tonight with Joey. I felt I owed you."

In that moment their relationship shifted. A bond of friendship grew, forged by a painful past. Entranced by his all-consuming look, she melted against the counter, her nerveless fingers releasing the towel to float to the floor.

He swallowed several times and dragged his gaze away. "Is there a Sunday school class that will help Joey?"

"There's one for the middle school kids. Andy belongs and loves it. It's a supplement to the youth group for that age."

"Then that's what I'll take him to."

"How about yourself? If you insist he go but you don't attend a class, won't that defeat your purpose?"

"Right. Do you go to one?" He stooped over and retrieved the towel from the floor, then handed it to her.

"A Bible study group."

"Is Kelli part of it?"

"No."

"Good."

"There's no way you can go to the church and Kelli not find out."

"I know, but I'd rather do this without getting her involved. She worries enough about me."

"Why does she worry?"

He raised one shoulder in a shrug. "She's my little sister."

"Maybe she senses something is wrong."

"Probably. We're only eighteen months apart and have always been close."

"When I was little, I used to wish I had a sister or brother, but now I'm glad no one else was affected by my mother."

"Is she still alive?"

Lisa grabbed a new clean dish towel and began drying the first washed pan. "No. She died of an overdose. After that I tried to get off the drugs, but it didn't work. I went cold turkey and it didn't last a day."

"It's hard to do it alone—actually, nearly impossible."

"We all need others." Her gaze snared his and held it for a long moment. *Let me help you.*

He finally broke visual contact with her and concentrated on the next pot, but she noticed his hands shook.

"I didn't get a chance to tell you last week at class, but I haven't had to force Andy to come. He wants to. He looks forward to coming," Lisa said the second David approached her at the refuge's recreational hall on the first Saturday in December.

"That explains his one-hundred-percent participation. That first lesson he hung back for half the class and got into the moves only at the end. Now he stands in the front line, eager to demonstrate if I need someone to."

"He hasn't said anything to me, but I think a weight has been lifted off his shoulders. How's Joey doing?"

"Last week he was much like Andy was that first lesson.

Today he participated more and what I saw was good. He's a natural like Andy. What I would love to do is pair them up. They would challenge each other."

"That's what I'm afraid of and the results wouldn't be pretty." She turned toward her son who came across the rec hall.

"Mom, can I go to the new barn with Gabe? I want to check on Tiger."

"Sure. I'll be over there in a minute. I haven't had a chance to see the barn since they moved the horses into it."

Andy jogged to catch up with Gabe who was leaving the building. Joey walked out behind the two boys at a slow pace.

"How's Joey getting along with the others?"

"Not so good. Roman tells me that he's hostile to most in his cottage." David strode toward the door. "I'd better make sure nothing happens outside. Joey was caught fighting on Monday again."

"Then is teaching him tae kwon do a good thing?"

"He needs discipline, confidence. All that anger is covering up a scared kid."

Outside David paused on the stoop. Lisa came up to his side. Andy and Gabe were nearly across the yard near the pasture that led to the barns. Joey stood still a few feet from the rec hall, his shoulders slightly hunched, staring at the ground as he kicked at some pebbles.

"Joey," Gabe called out.

Joey raised his head and stared at the two boys.

"Wanna come to the barn with us?"

Joey didn't say anything but turned away. Lisa caught the longing in his eyes that he quickly covered when he found her looking at him. "I don't like animals," he muttered and started toward his cottage, set off from the other four.

"You might not like animals, but Roman told me you're supposed to muck some stalls out after class." David descended the couple of steps.

"That's all there is here. Chores! I'm slave labor," Joey yelled.

"You're being clothed, fed and given a roof over your head, so doing a few chores isn't too much to ask."

Joey fisted his hands. "But I didn't ask to be here."

"Remember the jail tour? Is that where you want to end up?"

Joey's chin jutted out. "I won't go to jail. I'm too smart."

"You got caught, didn't you? If you keep doing the same thing, you're headed in that direction. People earn their way in this world." David turned back to her. "Want to walk with me to the barn?" He ambled across the yard with her next to him, glancing back halfway to the pasture. "I expect you to fulfill your duties as everyone does here at the refuge," David said to Joey who remained glued to the same spot.

Grumbling peppered the air behind Lisa. Joey was going to fight them every step of the way. "Mitch is worried about his brother. Joey won't even talk to him much. He thinks Mitch sold him out. It breaks my heart to see money and drugs possessing a child. As far as I'm concerned, Joey is still a child."

"It's happening younger and younger now. For the past two years I've avoided anything having to do with drugs if possible. That's the main reason I got my detective shield while I was still in Dallas. The area of town I patrolled was riddled with a drug problem." He stopped halfway across the meadow, turning toward her while he glanced behind him. "Now I see I can't run from my past. It just follows you wherever you go, so I've got to deal with it. I have you to thank for that shift."

"I did?" Lisa noticed Joey trudging toward them, slowing his pace when they halted.

"Kelli told me how you help some of the women at the shelter if they're having trouble staying off drugs. If you can face your past every time you work with others with a drug problem, then I can, too. I'm starting with Joey, but no telling where this new attitude will lead me."

"My, that sounds like optimism from you." She pressed her palm against his forehead. "Just checking for a fever."

His chuckles echoed through the pasture. "We'd better keep moving. I don't think Joey can go any slower and still be going forward if we don't."

"You know often when there is a child who's angry or withdrawn Peter or Roman have hooked them up with one of the abandoned animals. The child becomes totally responsible for that animal."

"That's a great idea. Isn't there a new potbellied pig someone dropped off the other day at the gate?"

"Yeah, Andy told me about it. Maybe Peter hasn't chosen anyone to name the pig yet. But there's also the litter of puppies and a couple of other animals."

At the old barn Lisa saw Peter talking with Roman in front of the stall that used to house Belle. The mare, along with her foal, Tiger, had been moved a few days ago to the new building. She headed straight for the two men in a serious discussion about the pig.

"Did Andy and Gabe go through here?" she asked, seeing the newest animal rooting around in the stall.

"Yeah. They went that way." Roman pointed toward the back of the barn.

David peered toward the front entrance. "I have a favor to ask. I'd like Joey to be responsible for one animal, its feeding, care, everything. Is that possible?"

"Sure. A lot of the kids take to a certain animal and end up taking care of it." Peter tapped his cowboy hat against his leg, then put it back on.

"Any suggestions?" David relaxed as Joey came into the barn.

"We've got several that are new. There's a litter of kittens that just arrived this morning, the puppies over there—" Roman waved his hand toward the pen that held them "—that pig behind us and a goat."

"After he mucks the stalls, have him do something with a couple of those animals and we'll see which one he responds to." David lowered his voice as Joey neared them. "We don't want him to know what we're doing. He'll fight us if he does."

"Sounds good to me." Roman faced the teen. "Joey, before you go to the other barn, please take the pig back to his pen. He got out and we found him in there." He gestured toward the stall. "Make sure he's secured. I'll be there in a sec to check the pen. We don't want him roaming around."

"Why not? He's just a pig." Joey's lower lip stuck out.

"Because dogs and pigs don't mix. A dog can be a predator, the pig its prey."

Joey stared at the animal making rooting sounds in the hay. "How am I supposed to get him?"

Roman walked to the tack room and returned with a leash. "Put this on him. He'll walk with you. He was someone's pet."

"Then why's he here?" Joey took the link of chain and collar.

Roman shrugged. "Someone left him on our doorsteps."

"He's been abandoned, the—" Joey snapped his mouth close.

"I thought you realized all these animals at one time were abandoned by their owners. We take them in and either keep them or find good homes for them."

Something softened in Joey's eyes for a few seconds before

he dropped his head, staring at the leash in his hand. Slowly he shuffled toward the stall. Lisa glimpsed him approaching the pig, mumbling something she couldn't hear clearly. Kneeling in the straw, the teen looped the collar around the animal's neck. The pig squealed but stood still while Joey sneaked a pat.

"I'd better get my toolbox and see what's wrong with the pen," Roman said as Joey led the pig out of the stall.

"We may have to move him into the stall if he keeps getting out. See you later. I'm heading into town to get feed." Peter ambled toward the entrance.

After the two men left, David turned toward Lisa. "I have courtside seats tonight at the university's basketball game. Do you and Andy want to come? I'm taking Joey. I'm hoping to give him a reason to want to get back on the team."

"Back on the team? Why after what he did?" All she could think of was the problems the teen caused her son.

"Because he needs a goal right now and the only thing he's expressed that he likes to do is basketball. He can't return without apologizing to his teammates, which I'm not sure he'll do. Please trust me. I won't put Andy in harm's way."

"You can't guarantee that."

David sucked in a deep breath. "Now who's cynical?"

"When it comes to my son, I have to look out for his welfare first."

"Joey needs people to care about him."

"And you think I should?"

"Not necessarily. I certainly understand if you don't want to go tonight." David rubbed the back of his neck, his gesture full of frustration. "I just thought Andy would enjoy seeing the game from courtside. I know the coach. We went to college together and played on the same team."

"Oh, you don't play fair. If Andy heard I refused that kind of offer, he wouldn't be pleased at all. They named the colt after the University of Cimarron City Tigers."

"I won't tell him I asked you."

Lisa stared toward the new barn off in the distance. "No, we'll go. I don't think Joey would do anything with both of us there. The charades game Thanksgiving evening went passively well. No blood was drawn, at least." She looked back at David. "There is a chance Andy won't want to go."

"Let's go ask him now before I say anything to Joey."

"There's also a chance Joey won't either."

"True, but I have a feeling he'll want to get out of his 'prison.'"

"You never told me how the jail visit went." Lisa strolled toward the back entrance.

"Okay. I'm not sure what effect it had on Joey. I had some of the prisoners talk to him about drugs. I showed him an inmate going through withdrawal, not a pretty sight. Joey grew very quiet after that, not that he was that talkative before."

"I could always talk to him," she said before she realized what she'd really offered to do—open herself up to a teen who had terrorized her son.

His gaze swept to her and he slowed his pace. "I can't ask you to do that. I have a feeling that wouldn't be an easy conversation for you."

He was right; it wouldn't be. She didn't think she would ever totally get over being ashamed of what she did as a youth. "He already knows I took drugs."

"But not the details. I can find others who are used to talking about it if I need to."

Lisa found Andy alone in the pasture behind the new barn with Tiger and Belle. "Where's Gabe?"

"He had to go home to eat lunch early." Andy ran his hand

down the colt's nose. "Mom, I'd like to stay this afternoon because we played our game last night. Is that okay?"

"Sure, but…" Her voice trailed off into the silence as she glanced at David.

He stepped forward. "I've got courtside tickets for the Cimarron Tigers' game tonight. Wanna go? I've invited your mom and Joey, too."

Andy frowned and averted his face, nuzzling it against the colt.

"Andy?" Lisa moved to the side and glimpsed the debate warring within her son. "It's your call."

"I guess."

David grinned. "Great, I'll pick y'all up. I'm glad you're coming. I know the coach, Andy. He said you could go to the locker room before the game if you wanted."

"He did?" Her son's expression brightened.

"Yup. Maybe even shoot some with them during the warm-up."

"You're kidding!" Andy threw his arms around the colt. "Tiger, did you hear what I get to do?"

"Hon, I'm leaving. I'll be back in a few hours to pick you up." Lisa headed toward the fence.

"Mom, I want to stay longer than that. Roman is going to give some of the animals their checkups. I want to help him. Coach, can you pick me up here tonight with Joey?"

"I can if it's okay with your mother."

"What about dinner?"

"I can always eat at Gabe's"

The eager expression on Andy's face was wonderful to see. She hadn't seen that enough lately with all that had been going on. "That's fine."

As she crossed the field with David next to her, hope blossomed in her. She was getting back the son she knew and also helping a friend. Now she understood where David was coming from. Although the killing of that thirteen-year-old was justified, he wasn't the kind of man who would take pleasure in it. In fact, it had affected him deeply and adversely. The scars ran deep, and she hoped she could help him heal. And maybe along the way also lend a hand to a child in need. She needed to find the courage to bare her soul to Joey, give him the disgusting details of what it was like to live a slave to drugs. Just as Joey's journey had become David's, so it would be hers, too.

Chapter Nine

Lisa flung the door to her apartment wide open, waving David inside. "Come in. I'm running late. It won't take me long to change."

"I'm a little early."

Lisa hurried into her bedroom and quickly changed into some jeans, light pink sweater and comfortable brown half boots with two-inch heels. Pausing at the mirror over the dresser, she ran a brush through her short hair, fluffed it some, then put on some lipstick on. As she left her room, she snatched up her brown purse.

Checking his watch, David whistled. "Under five minutes. I'm impressed. What have you been doing in here?" He gestured toward the stacked boxes in the middle of the living room.

"Getting my Christmas decorations down. Andy and I are getting our tree tomorrow after church. We always decorate the first weekend in December. Well, not always, but these past few years it has become our tradition." She made her way toward the door. "I have to admit this is our favorite time of year. How about you?" She remembered he'd told her once he didn't care for Christmas. Maybe she could find out why.

"Decorate? Never."

She slid a look toward him. "I guess not having children makes things different. Not even a little tree, a wreath, something?"

"Nope. I don't care for the holidays. The best I'll do this year is tolerate it because of Max and Abbey."

"How sad."

"The shooting with the teen occurred two years ago right after the holidays. Christmas last year brought it all back. I don't want that to happen again."

Maybe he needed to make new memories. That thought spurred an idea. "Andy and I could use some help chopping down a tree and getting it to the car."

"You're gonna chop down your own tree?"

"Yes. This is another tradition we started. Wanna come help us tomorrow?" Lisa locked her front door and headed toward the stairs leading to the ground level.

"I guess so. What did you do in the past?"

"Begged Noah or Jacob to help me. Last year Nathan at work did." She grinned at David. "I like to spread the wealth. You're this year's victim."

He laughed, opening his passenger side door for her. "Okay. I'll be your willing—victim." After he rounded the front of his Jeep and climbed into the vehicle, he asked, "Why do you cut down your own tree? All you have to do is go to one of the places that sell them and buy one. I believe they'll even load it into your car. Much easier."

"When Andy lived at the refuge, it was Christmastime. Hannah and Jacob took the kids into the field, they picked a tree, then Jacob chopped it down. Andy remembers that as the first real Christmas he had. I like to continue that feeling for him even if it's harder to do."

"Then I'll help any way I can. I do have fond memories of my childhood at Christmas. Kelli loves that time of year and forced me to participate as a child." David pulled his car out into the traffic.

"I can just see her twisting your arm."

His chuckles peppered the air. "Yeah and it hurt."

"On a different topic. How did Joey respond to the invitation to the game tonight?"

"With his usual blasé attitude. Actually blasé is a step up from his usual attitude."

"Ah, you're making progress, then."

"Inch by inch."

"Did Joey gravitate toward an animal today?"

David stopped at a light and looked over at her. "Would you believe the pig? I thought he would take to the litter of puppies or even the goat, but to my astonishment he helped Roman fix the hole the pig made under the fence during his 'great escape.' Roman overheard Joey muttering about wanting to make sure no dogs got it." When the light turned green, David pressed his foot on the accelerator. "Roman told Joey he could name the pig if he wanted."

"What did Joey say?"

"He'd think about it."

Quickly the town was left behind, and the neon brightness gave way to the dark landscape occasionally being punctuated with twinkling lights. David flipped on his radio, the station playing Christmas music.

When he started to turn it, Lisa asked, "Will you leave it on? I love Christmas music, and I start listening right after Thanksgiving."

"You don't get tired of it?"

"Nope. There are so many beautiful songs. This is one of my favorite." She closed her eyes and laid her head back, listening to the female vocalist sing, "What Child Is This?"

Ten minutes later David turned into Stone's Refuge and

pulled up in front of Joey's cottage. Lisa saw her son across the compound on Hannah's porch. When the Jeep stopped, he raced across the yard toward the vehicle.

"I'll be right back." David exited his car and hurried to the cottage.

Andy slid into the backseat. "I can't believe I'm gonna get to sit courtside at one of the Tigers' games. They are supposed to win their conference."

Excitement filled her son's voice and brought a grin to Lisa's mouth. "And you get to shoot baskets with them during the pre-game."

"Yeah. The only thing about tonight I don't like is who I have to share it with."

"Andy!" Earlier today she'd decided she needed to encourage her son to befriend Joey. The child needed reasons to seek a change. She knew that better than most. "Have you ever thought that just maybe Joey needs a true friend?" As she asked her son that question, thoughts of David instantly materialized in her mind. He needed one, too.

Andy remained silent as David and Joey got into the Jeep. Peering into the back seat, she noticed her son hugging the door, keeping his distance from Joey. The darkness hid Andy's expression, which she decided was probably a good thing. The wariness radiated from him as it did from Joey.

"Let's go. We should be there when the team comes out onto the court to warm up." David pulled away from the cottage. "Joey, have you decided if you're gonna name the pig?"

"I guess so. That way he won't be called some dumb name like Tiger."

Lisa tensed, biting the inside of her mouth. She held her breath waiting for Andy to lash out at Joey. Surprisingly, he continued to be quiet.

"Do you have a name picked out yet?"

From the tight sound of David's voice, Lisa realized he, too, was keeping his anger under wraps.

"Nope," Joey finally mumbled.

The rest of the trip to the arena seethed with silence, plausible and thick. It was going to be a long night, Lisa thought, if the start was any indication.

After parking the Jeep close to the building, David climbed from the vehicle with Andy and Joey hopping out the second the engine was switched off. As though they were in a race for the entrance, both boys rushed across the asphalt lot toward the bright lights of the arena. At a more sedate pace David followed with her beside him.

When Joey reached the double glass doors into the building and blocked Andy's entrance for a few seconds, David sighed. "I love a good competition, but I think Joey and Andy will be taking it a bit too far before this evening is over with."

Finally Joey burst through the doors with Andy on his heels. They weaved through the light crowd gathered early for the game, but both were halted by the usher who collected the tickets at the bottom of the escalator that led to the main floor. But not before Joey and Andy had managed to go ahead of some people.

"Guess they can't do much without these." David waved the set of tickets in the air, then pulled the door open for Lisa to enter the arena first.

"Good thing or we might not see them for the rest of the night. I have a picture of them racing from one point to the next, barely stopping long enough to catch their breaths."

When David reached the boys, he dragged them over to the side and let the other fans go ahead of them. "I think we need to establish a few ground rules before we go another step. If you two can't follow them, we'll leave immediately. No pre-game warm-ups, no courtside seats to watch the game. It's all in your control if we stay or leave."

Joey wrenched his arm from David's loose grasp, stuck out his lower lip and scowled at first David then Andy. Her son didn't do much better. He returned Joey's look with his own slicing one, his jaw set in rigidity as though they were drawing the line in the sand.

"Here's the deal. At all times you will *walk* from point A to point B. No cutting in line. We need to know where you two are. I will not chase after you." David took several steps toward Lisa, stopped and peered back at the still boys. "C'mon. Let's go or the warm-ups will start without you."

She had to work to get such firmness in her voice, but it came naturally to David. The two adolescents walked to the back of the short line. Lisa stood behind them, trying to suppress her grin.

David leaned close to her ear. "If they glare any harder at each other, their faces are going to permanently freeze in that expression. At least that was what my mother used to tell me when Kelli and I fought with each other."

His breath tickled her nape, and she shivered. "Then there's hope that Joey and Andy will actually say something civil to each other. You and Kelli are such good friends now."

When she'd been a little girl, she'd always wanted a little sister or even a brother. As she grew older, her longing multiplied. She'd so wanted an ally against the girls who bullied her, against her mother who alternated between neglecting her to trying to treat her as if she were a friend she could take drugs with. She'd begged the Lord for a sister or brother, for someone. Now she was glad she didn't have any siblings to share the kind of child-hood she'd had. Thankfully, God knew what He was doing.

David shuffled toward the usher at the bottom of the escalator. "Knowing Kelli loves and cares about me helps, but sometimes…" Silent, he looked around as though suddenly re-alizing they were in the middle of a crowd.

She wouldn't pursue the conversation now, but she would later. For just a second a twinge of hurt coated his words. It had to be connected to the shooting of the adolescent in Dallas. David was trying to be cynical and hardnosed, but she sensed deep inside him he wasn't. And that fact was tearing him apart.

David reached around Andy to hand the usher the four tickets. Her son started to bolt up the escalator when David cleared his throat. Andy glanced back and moved almost in slow motion, even letting Joey go first. He strutted past Andy.

David chuckled. "This is gonna be interesting."

"I'm not sure that's the word I would use." Lisa stepped on the stairs while watching the glowers return to both boys' faces.

"That went pretty well," Lisa murmured as Joey and Andy came off the court.

"Yeah, but neither one needs to sit next to each other." David watched the two as they talked with some of the players. "I was a little concerned when they both went up for the same ball."

"I visualized a tug-of-war that would end on the floor with them tumbling around in a big heap. I think number twenty-four had the same vibe. He snatched that ball from the air so fast the boys were stunned."

"I'll have to thank him later. I did let the coach in on the situation just in case something happened."

"And he still let Andy and Joey practice with the team. I'm gonna have to give him a hug and kiss after the game."

As the boys approached, David whispered, "If we last that long."

Joey sat on the left side of David while she positioned herself between him and Andy. "Did you have fun?" she asked her son.

"Yeah. They even invited me back for one of their practices during the week. Me, Mom." He tapped his chest. "Can I?"

The joy on her son's face thrilled her. "We'll work something out. Let me talk with David and make sure it's all right with the coach. We'll probably have to coordinate with Joey and his schedule at the refuge."

Andy peered around her at David and Joey. "Sure. I understand."

Then her son sat back and kept his gaze trained on the court, not saying a word to her through the whole first half. He leaped into the air and yelled at all the appropriate times, but some of the enthusiasm he'd had earlier deflated at the mention he might have to share the practice with Joey.

By the time the half neared, all Lisa wanted to do was get her son alone and try to explain her reasons for desiring Joey participate in the practice, too. The invitation was probably extended to Joey, anyway. At least she hoped so. He needed some things to look forward to. From Mitch she'd discovered that their mother had left them when Joey was only four. She got the feeling both of them had never had a woman doting over them. Not that she wanted to be Joey's mother, but he needed to know people cared about him. Watching him on the court with the Tigers and through the game, she'd realized that.

The sound of the horn announcing halftime blared through the arena.

Joey stood, wiggling. "I've got to go to the bathroom."

"Okay, I'll come, too." David started to rise.

"I can't even go to the bathroom by myself?" Joey's jaw firmed in a challenge. "Where am I gonna go? It's cold outside. You can hold my coat."

"Okay. The second half starts in twenty minutes." David took the heavy jacket and pulled his wallet out. "Why don't you get something to drink and eat while you're up there?"

Surprise widened Joey's eyes. He stared at the five-dollar bill David held out to him. After half a minute, he blinked, snatched the money and sidled toward the aisle. "Be back before half's over."

After Joey was gone five minutes, Andy turned to Lisa. "I need to go, too."

"Fine. Do you want anything to drink or eat?"

"Yeah, a drink. Can I bring you back something?" He leaned forward and spoke to David. "Or you?"

"I'm good," David said, glancing up the aisle.

"So am I." Lisa gave him some money.

David stood as Andy left. "I want to trust Joey, but he hasn't earned that yet. I'm gonna go to check and make sure everything is all right."

Have I earned it? Do you believe yet that I won't ever go back to drugs? "I'll go with you."

"I'm almost afraid to say this but the first half went well." David squeezed through a group coming down the stairs.

"If by well you mean the thick silence between Andy and me, then yeah, it went well."

"I noticed. I didn't want to say anything. I heard Joey's name, so I figured it was about him." David angled toward her, his gaze straying toward the entrance at the top of the stairs.

"Yes and no. Did you know some of the players asked Andy to come to one of their practices during the week?"

"I mentioned something to Coach Williams. I was hoping that was a possibility."

"Did Joey say anything to you?" Lisa asked, emerging out of the stands into the foyer that ringed the arena.

"Nope, but then he wasn't talking, either."

"Thankfully Andy and I are at least on speaking terms."

"After the game, I'll ask Brad about the invitation and see which day is the best."

Andy tore through a crowd standing in line to use the restroom, almost knocking down a woman in his haste.

"Andy, what are—"

"Mom, Joey's disappeared. I saw him with an older teen, I turned to pay for my drink and when I looked back maybe ten seconds later, he was gone from the other line."

David gaze fixed on the worry in Andy's face. "Can you show me where you last saw him?" He scanned the multitude still in the arena foyer.

Going against the stream of fans entering the seating area, Lisa followed David with Andy next to him. Near the concession stand close to their section, Andy pointed to the place where he'd last seen Joey. Their surroundings held only a few stragglers still in line for food.

"Andy, you stay here in case Joey comes back. Your mom and I will circle the arena." David gestured to his left. "Lisa, I'll go this way. You—" he waved his hand toward the right "—go that way."

As Lisa hurried around the outside ring that circumvented the basketball court, she checked any place that Joey might be. Up ahead a teen about sixteen or seventeen kept scanning the area, then peer back behind him. The hairs on her neck rose. A lookout? She could remember that happening many times when she would make contact with her drug dealer. One of his minions would keep watch for the police while he made the transaction with her. She slowed her pace, digging around in her purse for her compact. After passing the teen, still standing in the same spot, looking up and down, she pretended to go toward a set of restrooms nearby.

Flipping her powder open, she lifted the mirror and fluffed her hair while keeping an eye behind her. Out of the corner of her view she glimpsed Joey pinned up against a concrete wall while a bigger, brawnier teen had his arm across Joey's chest. The fury in the older boy's stance and gestures iced her blood. She snapped the compact closed, hiked her purse straps up higher on her shoulder and pivoted toward the lookout.

"Hey, maybe you could help me." She headed toward him while he backed away from where Joey and the other teen were. "I'm searching for my son. He's got away from me and I can't find him. Have you seen a—"

The older adolescent who had Joey trapped against the wall hurried from the dim alcove and away from his friend in the direction David would be coming. Lisa started backing toward the small hallway to check on Joey.

"I can't help you," the lookout mumbled and scurried after his friend.

Lisa didn't see much of the other teen. He had a hoodie on, masking part of his face. She watched a few more seconds, then spun around and hurried toward the alcove. In the half-light Joey, his face pale, sat on the floor, his back pressed against the concrete as if he'd slid down the wall. His gaze riveted to hers, and he immediately wiped all the fear from his expression. But she'd seen it.

"Who was that?" Lisa asked, hovering over the thirteen-year-old.

"No one." Joey shoved himself to his feet.

"Joey, I know what's happening here. Was that the person you got your drugs from?"

He thinned his lips together and scowled at her.

"You have people who care about what happens to you. Don't let drugs destroy your life like they almost did mine. There were times I was so out of it I didn't know it was night or day. I lived in a fog." Telling him about her experience opened a fissure of pain that threatened to swallow her. But she wouldn't stop if it would help Joey see the road he was taking. "All I wanted to do was find any means to get my next score. Is that the type of life you really want to live?"

Joey shrugged away from the wall. "I'm not a user like you were. I'm smarter than that." He started forward.

The child's words hurt, but she wasn't going to let his anger defer her from her course. She would continue to try and help him or anyone who needed it concerning drugs. Then perhaps what she'd done years ago would be put to a good purpose. That was how she lived with herself.

David came into the alcove, stopping Joey at its entrance. "What's going on?" David asked, thunder in his voice, his expression fierce.

Joey's eyes became slits. "Is it a crime now to talk with a friend?"

"Is that what you were doing? Why back here?"

"Maybe 'cause I like privacy. I don't have it at the pr— refuge." Joey paused a few feet from David.

"Privacy for what?"

"Nuthin'." Joey lowered his head.

"Empty your pockets inside out." After Joey complied, heated ice flowing off him in volumes, David said, "Lift your jeans."

After David checked to make sure Joey hadn't hidden anything in his socks, the boy muttered, "Satisfied? I don't have any drugs."

David nodded, allowing Joey to pass him. On the way back to their seats, Lisa with David hung back several feet from Joey. The adolescent went by Andy and mumbled something to her son she couldn't hear.

"What did he say to you?" she asked when she caught up with Andy.

"Snitch."

"Good thing you were. I'm not sure that was an amiable meeting between two friends. Did you know either teen?"

"No. Sorry, Mom. You think they were going to hurt Joey?"

She let David go ahead. "Yeah, maybe. You did the right thing, hon."

As Lisa made her way down the stairs to the floor of the basketball court, she couldn't shake the feeling that the teen with the hoodie had threatened Joey. She wished she'd gotten a better look at the adolescent's face because his swagger as he'd walked away reminded her of one of her drug dealers who'd thought he owned the world and no one could touch him. He'd ended up in prison.

After dropping both Andy and Joey at the refuge, David drove Lisa to her apartment. "Andy likes to stay out at the ranch."

"Yeah, it's like a second home to him. He's especially close with Hannah and Jacob, and of course, Gabe is his best friend."

"Too bad Gabe doesn't play basketball. He's really taken with tae kwon do."

"I've seen Andy practice in his room. He doesn't think I know, but he does almost every night."

David pulled into the parking lot at her place. "How do you think this evening went?"

"You know I expected Joey to be mad at Andy because he came and got us, but he was actually pretty civil the rest of the evening. He was scared. He wouldn't admit it, but I saw the fear in his eyes."

"I saw the teen you describe pass me, but I couldn't see his face, either. I wish I could ID him. He might be behind Joey selling the prescription drugs. I've never believed him when he told me he worked alone. I don't think he did."

"I agree. Very suspicious." She shifted toward him, the light from the building revealing the hard planes of his face. "Whoever he was, he went out of his way to hide his identity. Maybe I'll talk with Mitch and see if he knows who it could be. I'll describe his build. He might have come around to Joey's place before."

"I did some more digging into Mitch. He really is trying to turn his life around."

"He's always available to work when I need extra help. I can't fault him as an employee, and he's worried about his brother." She put her hand on the handle. "Do you want to come up? I made some cookies—ginger snaps."

David perked up, straightening in the seat. "That's my favorite."

"Yeah, I know. Kelli told me last weekend. I've had this recipe and thought I'd try making them. They aren't too bad, according to my son."

"Then I've got to try one or maybe two or three."

She opened the door. "C'mon, then. Actually I wouldn't mind a cup of decaf." What he didn't know was that she intended to get to know him better. While baking the cookies last night, she'd planned her strategy. She'd wow him with the delicious-tasting ginger snaps, then zap him with questions about his life in Dallas. She wanted to understand him so she could help him.

Yeah, right. That was the only reason she'd stayed up late baking the cookies. Or quizzing Kelli about what David liked. It wasn't because she was interested in him as a man. *Okay, I am very interested in David. And I know I'm setting myself up to be hurt.*

After she put the coffee on to brew, she retrieved the cookies and placed the plate on the kitchen table. "Have you gotten any good leads concerning that robbery gang that struck The Ultimate Pizzeria? I've read a few stories in the paper, but they didn't tell me much."

"Yeah, they're eager to point out the police's lack of stopping this gang."

"Something will break on the case. Sit. I'll pour us some coffee."

"There goes your Pollyanna outlook again."

"It's better than being a Grinch."

"Ouch. I think that was pointed at me and my lack of enthusiasm for Christmas. Remember I'm helping you tomorrow with the tree. That should count for something."

"Only if you stay and help Andy and I decorate it."

His eyes widened. "Ms. Morgan, I do believe you're blackmailing me."

She thumped her chest. "Who, me?"

"Yes, ma'am, you." He took a ginger snap and began chewing it. "Mmm. Very tasty. Better than my mom's which is saying a lot."

Turning her back to him, she filled two mugs with the rich black liquid, its aroma wafting about her. She swept around to head to the table and nearly stumbled into David positioned right behind her with a cookie, one bite taken from it, in his hand. Quickly she steadied herself to keep from sloshing the coffee.

David plucked one mug, then the other from her and set both of them on the counter along with the half-eaten cookie. "Why would Kelli tell you I love ginger snap cookies?"

He was too close for her peace of mind. His familiar scent swirled about her, mingling with the smell of coffee that hung in the air. "It just came up in conversation." She pretended a fascination with the mug nearest her.

"It did? Why were you two discussing me?" He stepped even closer.

Her heartbeat thumped against her chest. She finally looked into his eyes. "If you must know I wanted to know more about you." There, she'd admitted her interest in him. "That's something friends do. Get to know each other."

Another few inches closer. He framed her face. "So that's what we are. I guess being friends is safer…" He let the rest of his sentence dissolve into silence.

Slowly he bent toward her, giving her plenty of time to pull away if she chose. She didn't. Her gaze fastened on his mouth as the thundering pounding of her heart drowned out all sound. His lips settled over hers, his fingers slipping through her hair. Then he wound his arms around her and drew her against him. His kiss deepened as though he intended to wipe any memory of another man from her mind. And he was succeeding.

When he parted, his breathing shallow, he still kept her caged against him. "This doesn't feel like friends." The huskiness of his voice demonstrated how affected he was by the kiss.

It matched her reaction. "No," she whispered, her voice barely working.

That was what scared her. She'd been lousy at relationships in the past, and she wasn't going to put Andy through a series of boyfriends ever again. And this particular relationship hadn't been without its obstacles. Pushing back from him, she encountered the stove and moved to the side to put space between them.

"I'd better go. We can arrange a time for me to help you cut down your Christmas tree tomorrow at church." He grabbed several cookies from the plate on the table. "Thanks for these. I haven't had any in a while. It brings back fond memories of my childhood and the holidays." Then without another word, he quickly made his way toward the front door.

Grasping the plate of cookies, Lisa hurried after him, but he was halfway down the stairs to the parking lot before she reached the balcony outside. She'd wanted him to have them. Tomorrow she would make her feelings clearer to him. Her stepping away might have signaled to him her disinterest. The hard part was she needed to figure out between now and then what exactly she wanted from him.

Chapter Ten

"This is the biggest tree ever!" Andy held the top part of the pine while David gripped the trunk.

Lisa rushed to unlock her front door and open it for them. "I hope it fits in the stand we have."

Andy peered back at David. "Mom's gonna make some hot chocolate, and she baked a cake last night."

David arched an eyebrow. "Baking two nights in a row?"

"I like to bake when I get the chance."

"She tells me she likes to when she needs to do some thinking."

Heat suffused her face at her son's explanation, which was true. She'd spent a good part of the night before trying to figure out what she wanted in a relationship with David. She kept thinking about how perfect Hannah and Jacob's relationship was. She wanted that and had never thought that would be a possibility. David revived that dream. He knew about her past and still kissed her last night. But what if it really didn't mean anything to him? What if—

"Mom—" Andy waved his hand in front of her face to get her attention "—where do you want the tree to go this year?"

Her blush deepened, searing her cheeks. She whirled away

from both of them and scanned her living room. "I guess over by the window so people can see the lights lit up at night."

David headed toward the spot she indicated. "Sounds like a good place to me. Where's the stand?"

"It's right here." Lisa rummaged through a box sitting on the couch and produced the item. "What do you think? Will it fit?" She set it on the carpet before the floor to ceiling window.

After David fit the stand on the base of the trunk, then tightened the screws to hold the tree in place, he straightened and stepped back. "Well, does it look okay?"

Lisa studied the pine that leaned to the left by at least fifteen degrees. "You don't do this often, do you?"

"I have to admit I don't normally go around chopping down trees, hauling them to my house and putting them upright in a stand. What's wrong?"

Andy giggled. "It's not straight."

"That's easy to take care of. I'll just—" David scooted it around "—turn it a little and you won't be able..." A frown twisted his mouth as he tilted his head to one side, then the other.

"It's worse. There's a hole in the back of the pine." Lisa stifled a smile as David moved the tree again.

"Why didn't you notice this hole when you were picking it out?" David rubbed his chin.

"I like a tree that's not perfect." Like her. She hadn't wanted it to be left at the Christmas tree farm. It needed a home, too.

"Okay, Andy, let's saw the bottom some to compensate for the leaning."

"We don't have one," her son said.

"You don't. What tools do you have?"

"A screwdriver and hammer. That's it." Lisa walked to the pine and turned it back the way it was. "Let's leave it like it is. It's growing on me. Perfect is overrated."

"If you're sure."

Andy nodded while she said, "Yes."

"What's next?" David stood back next to her and again studied the pine. "Lights, ornaments, tinsel?"

"We put the lights on after I check to make sure they're working." Andy dug into another box on the coffee table and pulled out several strings of multicolored twinkling lights.

"While you two get those up, I'll go make the hot chocolate and bring the cake in here."

"She makes it from scratch. It's great!" Andy plugged in the first string.

"Yeah, she is," she heard David murmur, thankfully too low for her son to hear as she passed David to go into the kitchen.

She shed her heavy sweater, the temperature in the apartment unusually warm. She checked to make sure her son hadn't turned up the thermostat. But the setting of sixty-eight mocked her. She quickly put the chocolate on to melt. While it was, she scalded some milk with vanilla flavoring in it and then dissolved sugar and salt in the hot liquid. The sweet mixture spiced the air as she poured it into the melted chocolate, then beat it with a whisk. When she was finished with making the hot chocolate, she filled three mugs, topping them off with whipping cream.

As she sliced the cake, she thought about baking it the night before. She was going to see where this situation—no, there wasn't a better word than relationship—went with David. If it was only friendship, then she would cherish that. If it was something more, then she wasn't sure what she would do, but she couldn't turn her back on David. She couldn't help him if she didn't invest some emotions into what was developing between them. She would place exactly what in the Lord's hand.

As she brought the large tray containing the mugs and cake into the living room, the sound of her son's laughter only confirmed what she had decided. David was a good man although he was too hard on himself and his experiences had jaded him. Andy was growing to like him and respect his opinion, which said a lot because he'd always been so standoffish where the police were concerned.

"I notice your mom waited until we were through with putting the lights on before coming back."

"Yeah, Coach, you're right." Andy's eyes gleamed with merriment.

"I think we should sit and enjoy the hot chocolate and cake while she puts on all the ornaments."

After she set the tray on the empty end of the coffee table, she fisted her hands and placed them at her waist. "This is what I get after slaving over the stove to fix this." She swept her arm wide above the goodies. "I can tell when my hard work isn't being appreciated so I guess—" she bent to pick up the tray "—I'll take this—"

David's hand closed around her nearest one and stilled her movements. "Put that way I think Andy and I can help you with the decorations while drinking our chocolate and eating our cake."

She grinned. "That's better." She passed one mug to Andy and another to David, then lifted her own into the air. "Here's to family and friends."

Andy and David took a sip of their drink, then placed their mugs on the tray and reached for the same slice of German chocolate cake, as though they were in sync with each other.

"Later," Lisa said, moving the cake away from both of them. Laughter bubbled up in her at the sight of the white mustache above their lips.

"What's so funny?" David looked at Andy, his brow creased. When the boy glanced David's way, he chuckled. "Never mind. I think I know."

Transfixed, David's gaze trained on her, Lisa watched him run his forefinger across his mouth, erasing the white whipping cream. All she could think about was those lips had been on hers the night before. Even after being exhausted staying up late to bake the cake, she couldn't rid her mind of the image of David leaning slowly toward her, a softness in his blue eyes that melted her insides like the gas flame melted the chocolate earlier.

She absently fumbled for her mug and took a swig, the warm liquid sliding down her throat, her gaze still locked with David's. His eyes sparkled as he dropped his attention to her mouth. He reached out toward her and brushed the pad of his thumb across her upper lip, then brought it to his mouth and sucked off the whipping cream.

Sensations—all centered on David—closed her throat, making it even difficult to pull air into her lungs. Her pulse raced while the temperature in the room skyrocketed.

"Mom, do I still have a mustache?"

Lisa blinked, suddenly remembering her son was in the room, not far from her and David. Again the heat of a blush colored her cheeks. How could she forget that even for a few seconds?

She wrenched her attention from David and focused on Andy. "No," she managed to say although she heard the squeak in her voice and winced.

"Are you okay, Mom?" Puzzlement entered her child's eyes.

"I'm fine. Let's get those ornaments on the tree," she muttered, turning away from both of them.

"Why can't we have our cake? I've got a craving for something—sweet," David said, amusement lacing his words.

She shot him a look she hoped squelched his humor. He might have the fine art of flirting down; she didn't. "That's your reward when we're through."

David peered at Andy. "Is she always such a hard taskmaster?"

Her son nodded. "Yup, when she has her mind set on something."

David clasped Andy's shoulder. "Well, then, let's get this done so we can play."

"Joey told me before class today that he's named his pig Bolt because it's always getting out. He said that yesterday they moved Bolt to a stall to see if that makes a difference." David took her hand as they walked behind Joey, Andy and Gabe toward the barn at the refuge on Saturday morning.

"I like that name." His fingers clasped around hers felt right.

"I think the Seven Step Program of Healing Joey's going through is starting to work. He doesn't seem as angry as he was a few weeks ago." Something out of the corner of her eye caught her attention. She scanned the meadow but couldn't find anything out of the ordinary.

"Yeah, I hope. But as you probably know, often a person will backslide."

"I'm living proof of that. But I did overcome in the end."

"Maybe I should go through that healing program Joey's doing because what I'm doing isn't working. I thought the move to Cimarron City was just what I needed. I thought changing jobs within the department was what I needed. Neither has taken the pain away, made me forget what happened in that alley."

The honor she experienced at being the one he told his troubles to filled her heart with an emotion she was afraid to feel. But in that moment her love for him bloomed. She wanted to take his pain into her, having been in the same low spot once in her life. Lisa halted, causing David to stop, too. She drew him back toward her and clasped his upper arms, looking into the vulnerability etched into each of his features. "Sometimes you can't do it alone."

"Is this where you tell me to turn it over to the Lord?"

"I could and you should, but I was going to tell you I'll listen anytime you're willing to talk. Keeping the poisonous thoughts bottled up inside you usually only means it eats away at you."

He brushed her hair behind her ears, one finger grazing down her jaw before tracing her mouth. "You make me think it's possible."

"It is. That's what I love about Christmas. It reminds me all things are possible through our Lord. Christmas was when I hit my lowest and started fighting my way up. When God sent us His only Son, He was sending us hope."

David leaned forward, his lips caressing hers. When he pulled back, his gaze, full of appreciation, captured hers. "I'm actually looking forward to the holidays this year. I might even get a small tree for my apartment."

"Be still, my heart. You get a tree? Did I hear correctly?"

He chuckled. "I know. It's a novel idea, but I enjoyed decorating yours last weekend."

"We can help you decorate yours."

He anchored her against him. "How about one evening just you and I decorate it?"

"Hmm. That's a possibility."

"I could even fix some dinner."

"You cook?"

One of his eyebrows rose. "Of course. Well, not great, but it's passable."

"How about I help with the cooking, too?"

"You've got yourself a date. Next Saturday night?"

"I may have to work until seven, but otherwise, yes." Lisa peered toward the barn. "I guess we should see where the boys went."

As they started forward, the potbellied pig called Bolt bolted from the back entrance with Joey chasing him.

"I think the pig got out again," David said with a chuckle.

Andy near the paddock where Belle and Tiger were turned toward the squealing sound. Suddenly from the other side of the barn a big cinnamon brown dog with white splotches darted toward Bolt, intercepting the pig in its flight.

"Get away!" Joey screamed, rushing the dog.

The stray held down Bolt. The pig's shrills sent chills down Lisa. She raced toward the foray with David a few feet in front of her. Andy, closer than they, also charged the attacking dog.

Her son and Joey arrived at the same time. Shouting, Joey yanked at the stray while Andy pulled Bolt from under the dog. As David reached the boys, the animal, a boxer, ran off.

Joey hurried to Bolt, red covering the animal's side. Tears streamed down the boy's face. "Is he dead?"

Andy looked up. "No, but we need to get Roman."

David stooped by the pig. "Andy, can you go get Roman? I saw his van at the cottage."

Her son leaped to his feet and raced toward the refuge across the meadow.

Lisa knelt on the other side of Bolt, checking the damage the stray did to the pig. "The wounds don't look too deep. He'll be okay, Joey."

"He's got to be. He's got to be." Joey sat near the pig's head, stroking it over and over. "You can't die."

When Roman arrived ten minutes later, Lisa and David pulled Joey back to let Roman tend to Bolt.

"It's my fault. I opened the door too wide. He got away from me before I could catch him." Joey's eyes glistened.

Andy, a little out of breath, came over to Joey. "You did what you could. Bolt likes to run. I think he likes to be chased. He thinks it's a game."

"I was gonna play with him. That's why I came to the barn. He should have stayed. He'll be all right. He'll…" Joey's words choked to a spattering end.

"Maybe he needs a friend." Andy's attention fixed upon Roman as he worked on the pig.

"I'm his friend." Joey stepped toward Roman, hovering near the vet, watching every move.

"We might be able to find him another pig to keep him company when you aren't around, Joey," Roman said, lifting his gaze to the teen nearby. "He's going to be fine. I'm going to take him to my practice and clean and stitch him up. I could use your help with Bolt. Okay?"

"Yes, anything."

Andy moved forward. "I can help, too."

"Good. I'm going to go get my van and then we'll load him in it. You two stay and keep him company." Roman rose.

Roman came to Lisa and David. "Keep an eye out in case that stray returns. No one was bit, were they?"

While Lisa said, "No," David shook his head.

"Good. Then we don't need to worry about rabies with y'all. We need to contact Peter, find that stray and make sure it isn't around here to do harm to other animals."

"We'll do that after you leave. I don't want the boys to worry about other pets getting hurt." Lisa scanned the area, checking to make sure the pens around them with various animals were secured and the pets safe.

"I'll be back in a minute." Roman loped across the meadow.

Listening to Joey's murmurs to Bolt tugged at Lisa's heart. "I thought a little while ago I saw something coming from the woods. We should check there first."

"Yes, but how are we going to capture the dog?"

Lisa backed up a few more paces so the boys couldn't hear what they were saying. They didn't need to worry about anything but Bolt. "Peter has a gun that shoots tranquilizers. We'll probably need that."

"Has Peter ever turned an animal away?"

"A couple of times if they might harm the ones here." Seeing her son comforting Joey caused her throat to constrict.

"Did you see the dog's ribs? It hasn't eaten much lately."

"Yeah, that makes for a dangerous animal." Again Lisa searched her surroundings, noticing Roman's van coming down the road toward the barn. "I'm thankful that Joey and Andy didn't get bit. They didn't think twice about coming to Bolt's aid."

"A month ago I would have been surprised by that from Joey, but in the past couple of weeks that pig has become important to him. Roman told me the other day Joey does what he has to at the cottage and in the program because then he gets to spend more time at the barn, which means more time with Bolt."

Roman backed up his van to the front entrance of the barn, then hopped from it and hurried toward them. He gave Bolt a shot, then spread a plastic sheet on the ground. After moving the pig to the sheet, Roman with David's help carried the animal to the van. Settling Bolt in the back with Andy and Joey on either side of the pig, Roman gave them some instructions, then closed the doors.

"Find the stray if possible. I'll take care of Joey and Andy and bring them back to the refuge." Roman climbed behind the steering wheel and started the engine.

Watching the van disappear from view, Lisa reached for David's hand. His strong grasp comforted her. She didn't relish looking for the stray, but it had to be done.

"We'd better call Peter. We don't want a repeat of earlier," David said.

"I know you're right, but the dog was only trying to survive."

"Maybe Peter will have a place for the stray other than here."

Lisa turned toward David. "Maybe. Or maybe it's lost and we find its owner. It looked like a pure-bred boxer."

"That's what I like to see—your Pollyanna outlook." A teasing glint shone in his blue eyes. "Let's go get Peter."

Five hours later, exhausted, Lisa sat at the kitchen table at Hannah's house. She nursed a lukewarm cup of coffee while waiting for a call from Peter telling her the fate of the stray boxer they found.

"They should be back soon." Hannah set her mug on the table.

"I hate this waiting." Lisa could still see the tears in Joey's and Andy's eyes as they left with Roman and Bolt in the van.

A sound from the front of the house announced the arrival of someone.

"Maybe that's good news, and they found a place for the boxer." Lisa cradled her drink in her hands to warm her cold fingers. "He must have been on his own for quite a while. Poor thing."

"Didn't I tell you, Peter. Lisa is always full of hope that things will work out," David said from the doorway into the kitchen. He grinned. "And they did. The boxer has a new home with a shop owner who needed a guard dog. The man had been into the shelter earlier today and asked the attendant to call if any dog came in that fit his needs."

"What a wonderful Christmas gift. Everything ended well because Roman said that Bolt would be back to one hundred percent in a week or so. He'll keep him overnight at his practice, but the pig should be back in his pen by tomorrow." Lisa rose. "It's cold out there. Want a drink of coffee?"

"Sounds good." David shed his heavy coat and draped it over the back of a chair.

Peter shook his head. "I'm heading home. Has Roman returned yet?"

"He should be here any minute." Lisa picked up the pot and poured some coffee for David.

When she sat next to David at the table, Lisa saw the tired lines in his face. It had been a long afternoon hunting down the stray dog, combing the whole ranch. She slid her hand to his and covered it. His gaze snagged hers. A slow smile blossomed in those blue depths. He mouthed the word thanks.

A door slammed at the front of the house.

Andy hurried into the room. "He's gonna make it. Roman is great!"

Shortly after that declaration, Roman entered, chuckling. "I need Andy to go before me and proclaim that more often."

"Where's Joey?" David asked as he took a sip of coffee.

"He went to his cottage. He didn't want to be late for dinner." Roman jiggled his car keys. "And I'd better not stay. I'm sure Cathy's wondering what's taken so long."

"Yeah, Mom. I'm hungry, too. We worked up quite an appetite today. I got to help Roman with Bolt. So did Joey."

"We'll grab something on the way home." Lisa remembered the plans she had made with David for next Saturday night. She glanced toward him and found his gaze on her, the glittering look in his eyes indicating he remembered, too.

David swallowed some more of his drink, then stood. "I'll walk you two to your car at the rec center."

Andy ran ahead of them as she and David left Hannah's after their goodbyes. Halfway across the compound David stopped and looked up at the black sky with a few shining stars. As they stood there more lights popped into view in the darkness above them. With a shiver of cold, she stuffed her hands into her pockets.

Finally David swung his gaze to her. "I prayed today for the first time in a long while."

"You did?"

"And He answered me. At the shelter it didn't look good for the boxer. I was sure they would have to put him down. The place is crowded with animals abandoned or lost from their owners. The clerk manning the counter didn't offer any hope because of what the dog had done. Then an attendant came from the back and told us about the machine shop owner who wanted a big dog to guard his place at night." David settled his hands on her shoulder. "God answered my prayer." His joy bubbled from him, spilling over into his expression and voice.

"I'm so glad, David."

"I've seen so much bad as a police officer. People and animals abused and abandoned. When I saw the boxer up close after Peter tranquilized him in order to capture him, I just didn't want this to end badly like so many other situations I've been in." He moved so close their lengths touched. "I needed hope things can work out good. Getting to know you has given me that ray of hope I've needed. Thank you, Lisa, for that."

David brushed his mouth over hers, once, twice, then settled into a deep kiss that rocked her. His need mingled with hers, radiating through her as though a star had come down from the sky and flowed through her veins.

Chapter Eleven

"You call this a tree?" Lisa fluttered her hand toward the fake pine, no more than two feet tall, sitting on a round table in front of the window that overlooked the parking lot.

"I like to ease into things," David said with amusement tinging his voice as he shut the door to his apartment Saturday night.

"How about if you ease any more your tree will disappear?"

He splayed his fingers over his chest. "I'm wounded. I took care picking this one out at the store."

"How much time? Five seconds?" Lisa dropped her purse in the chair near her and removed her overcoat.

"I got some ornaments and a string of lights while I was at the store, too."

"That's good. Otherwise we wouldn't have anything to decorate the tree with."

"I think I hear sarcasm in your voice."

"Bingo. You are astute." Laughter bubbled from her. She couldn't contain it any longer. "You really are hopeless when it comes to celebrating Christmas."

"I got tinsel, too." David shook the small oblong box with a picture of silver tinsel on its front.

"Where are the ornaments you got?" Lisa tossed her coat over her purse, making a slow turn as she surveyed David's apartment. Sterile, very little to indicate the man who lived here. "You've been in Cimarron City for almost five months now?"

"Yeah. Why?"

"Not many personal touches." She swept her arm to indicate the room she stood in the middle of. No pictures on the walls, books in the nearly empty shelves, magazines stacked near his lounge chair, photos adorning the tables scattered about or knickknacks that pointed out who the man was.

"I'm not here that much."

"Then why bother with this—tree?"

"Because I wanted to show you I was trying to get into the holiday spirit."

You did? His statement surprised her. "I don't want you to do it for me. I want you to do it for yourself. And really the tree isn't 'getting into the spirit.'" She covered the short distance between them and laid her hand over his heart. Its beat hammered against her palm, making her vividly aware of David and that they were alone. "Your Christmas spirit comes from within." She tapped her finger against his chest. "From here. It's a state of mind, not decorations."

"And I've failed?"

He gave her a little boy look that sparked her laughter. "Let's just say you're a work in progress, and I have my work cut out for me."

He dug into his jeans pocket and withdrew his keys. "Then let's go to the store and buy a bigger tree. More ornaments. Another box of tinsel and more strings of lights."

She shook her head. "You aren't getting the point. That won't make you get into the mood."

"What will?"

"Actually you've been doing it—helping others."

"Then why did you agree to come help me decorate my tree?"

"Think about that."

Both of his eyebrows rose. "Helping—me?"

"Yes. Let's take care of this tree, eat dinner, then I have something we can do that always puts me in the mood."

David moved closer, gathering her to him. "What?"

"A surprise."

"What if I can't wait?"

"Tough, you're gonna have to. That's all I'm gonna say on the subject." She pretended to be zipping her mouth.

He snuggled her against him, bending forward until his lips touched her ear. "There's nothing I can do to convince you to change your mind and at least give me a little hint what's in store?"

His whispering, enticing and playful, tempted her. "Okay, I'll tell you one thing. We're going to the mall to see Santa." Hopefully he would relent his particular brand of persuasion.

Then he nipped at her lobe. "I'm too big to sit on Santa's lap."

She wanted to laugh at the image that unfolded in her mind, but she was too busy melting at nibbles on her ear. If she hadn't been clutching David, she would have wilted to the floor. "That won't be required," she murmured.

Finally he drew back, giving her some breathing room. "I guess the only thing we can do is get this tree taken care of, eat dinner and go to the mall. You're a tough one, Lisa Morgan. I used my best technique on you."

She pulled away, sucking in a lungful of air. "And I thought I was special." She spun around to put more distance between them, so she could think straight.

But David spun her back toward him. He framed her face, forcing her to look deep into his eyes. "Oh, there's no doubt in my mind. You are special to me, and that may be the problem."

She stiffened. "Problem? I think your persuasive technique just did a nosedive."

His hands fell away from her. "Have you ever thought about what a pair we make? Two wounded people trying to heal. I have to admit you're farther along than me, but we have so much against us."

Yes, she realized that, but she couldn't shake the feeling the Lord wanted her right where she was—with David. Perhaps only to help him, but what if He wanted more than that?

"We're here," David announced at the mall near the area where Santa was seeing the children.

Lisa made her way toward the front of the line waiting to see Santa and said something David couldn't hear to the assistant, dressed in a pine green elf suit with bright red trim. Then Lisa approached Santa who beamed at her and even winked. Next he pulled out an envelope and gave it to her. She smiled and waved goodbye, then ambled back to him.

"I've got it. Let's go." She sent him a saucy smile.

"Got what? Go where?"

"Why, shopping, of course!"

"Shopping! You know the thing I avoid worse than Christmas is shopping."

"Well, I'm about to change your mind." She flapped the envelope in the air as she headed toward a large department store, leaving him watching her disappear among the perfume counters.

He hurried his pace to keep up with her, the cloy scents of various fragrances assailing his nostrils as he followed her trail through the maze of displays to the children's department. Stopping in the middle of the young girls' clothes, Lisa began checking out the dresses.

He came up to her side. "What's going on?"

"What's it look like? I'm shopping."

"Yeah, I see that. Why now?"

She faced him, her lips twitching with humor, her eyes sparkling with mischief.

"Okay, you've had your fun. Are you ready to go?"

Her laughter escaped. "You don't go with the flow much, do you?"

"Order is important."

"Yes, I agree, but flexibility is so much more important. It keeps your blood pressure down."

"Mine isn't up." Although on second thought, if he checked it at the moment, it might have risen some. All these female clothes choked the very air he breathed.

"You look trapped."

"Yeah, hence the comment about not liking to shop."

"Tonight we're not shopping for us or even our loved ones. We're buying for some children who don't have anything for Christmas. I have a list of five names. One I pay for, but the others are from the collection we took up at work."

That statement cut the wind out of his sails. He'd been about to protest and tell her he would meet her at his car. But her beautiful expression, full of excitement and happiness, appealed to him. He wanted that.

"Santa gave you the names?"

"Yes, he volunteers at a charity. He's retired and goes to our church. He's been doing Santa here at the mall for the past few years." She gave him the envelope with the list of names and items requested.

"There's only toys on the list."

"I know. I always threw in some clothes, too. These children need those, too. They just don't think about that. I usually bring Andy, but I asked him if I could bring you this year."

"And he gladly stepped aside." David chuckled. "Smart guy. I doubt he likes to shop anymore than me. How about just giving them money? Wouldn't that be easier?"

Her mouth twisted into a frown. "That's not what this outing is about. It's about giving our time and thought to what another might want or need. It's about giving something of ourselves to another. That's part of what Christmas is about. Christmas is Jesus' birthday, and He gave Himself for our salvation." She turned back to the rack of clothes. "I could use your help picking out some clothes for the boys. That's usually Andy's job. He insisted on that a couple of years ago when I put together an outfit that made him cringe."

"Where do I go?" David scanned what seemed like miles and miles of racks of clothes.

"The boys' section is at the other end." Lisa pointed toward the area. She showed him the list again with the sizes next to the children's names, took out a pen and wrote down some items of clothing next to the boys' names. "This is what I need for them." She tore the bottom part and gave it to him. "If I get through before you, I'll come down there and help."

David trudged toward the other end. When he needed new clothes, he ran into a store and grabbed whatever he found first that fit and left as fast as he could. That was what he would do.

But when he reached the boys' department, a sea of clothes greeted him. He peered at the list clutched in his hand.

A coat first. I can do this. He managed to find the racks of coats. Heavy or light? What color? What size? Ah, a six and eight. I can do this.

He waded through the racks until he found the one with the sizes he needed. As he stared at the different colors and types, Christmas music filtered into his thoughts from the sound system piped into the store. Suddenly he stopped and listened to the words about giving people faith and a place to be safe. He looked again at his list and realized these children he was shopping for might not have that. He'd certainly seen that in his job. Was the Lord the light, a beacon to a place where they could be safe? Lisa felt so, had experienced it in her life.

As he inspected each garment for the two boys on his list, his spirits lightened. He decided to throw in a few more extra items a kid might like. Whistling to the different carols, he finished his task and went to pay for the clothes. This was his treat.

"You didn't have to follow me home," Lisa said when she got out of her white Chevy at her apartment.

"Yes, I did." David rounded the front of his Jeep. "You'll need help carrying the presents upstairs. And how about wrapping all these gifts? That'll be a big job."

"Andy is home from Gabe's by now. He can help. Unless you'd like to."

"I started a job and I want to finish it."

Lisa popped her trunk. "You aren't tired from shopping?"

"Yeah, but I'll recover. Honestly, though, I don't know how people can do that all day. It's hard work."

"I'll make some hot chocolate, and I have some chocolate chip cookies I made yesterday evening. That's Andy's favorite, but I'm sure he'll share with you." She piled his arms with packages. They had been able to buy more than she'd thought, mainly because David had contributed, doubling their amount. After she grabbed some bags, she shut her trunk. "So tell me what you thought of shopping tonight once you got past the horror of being in the middle of a department store."

"Not bad. I'd help you next year."

Next year. Where would they be this time next year?

Friends? More? The smile she'd seen on David's face as they'd picked out the requested toys and even added a couple more to the short list gave her hope. He'd enjoyed himself.

"I'll come back and get the rest of the gifts." David balanced his load and pushed the bell with his elbow.

When Andy opened the door, he grinned. "Boy, there's a lot to wrap."

"Yeah, but we have another helper." Lisa entered her apartment.

Andy took some of her packages and put them on the floor. "Are there any more in the car?"

"Yes, if you help, we can do it in one trip."

While her son accompanied David downstairs, Lisa retrieved the wrapping paper, scissors, tape and bows from the closet. Then she went into the kitchen and made hot chocolate and pulled out the cookies. When she carried the goodies into the living room, she found Andy and David already wrapping presents.

When David completed his first gift, he held it up. "I'm not very good at this."

Andy burst out laughing when he saw the box with part of its white surface showing, the crinkled paper taped with enough for three packages.

David frowned. "Okay, this isn't the best I've seen. I always have someone at the store wrap my gifts."

"I can see why," Andy said, chuckling.

That set the mood for the rest of the wrapping. Lisa showed David what to do step by step, but he was still all thumbs. Andy took his gifts and straightened them the best he could, but she wouldn't stop David from participating. His smile and stories of how he would con his sister into doing his shopping and wrapping as a child were exactly what she'd wanted, especially because she didn't have warm memories of her own to share.

David needed to see how being around family and friends could change his feelings concerning the Christmas season.

An hour later Andy put the last present on top of a stack, one of several that littered her living room. He yawned and stretched. "'Night, Mom, Coach."

Lisa rose and gathered up the empty mugs and plate of cookies. "Be right back." After she placed the dishes in the sink, she turned to go back into the living room.

David stood in the entrance, his intense gaze fastened onto her. "Thank you, Lisa, for this evening."

"I should thank you. You had me over for dinner."

"I can't remember having this much fun at Christmas in years. I get the point about going out yourself and buying the gifts for others less fortunate. I've always just given money at this time of year and never thought beyond that. This means more to me. It makes each gift we bought special." He crossed the room and tugged her against him. "I won't forget what you shared with me tonight."

She couldn't reply. His words swelled her love for this man so much that her throat jammed with the emotions she was experiencing. All she could do was stared at the tenderness in his eyes.

Cupping her face, he planted his mouth over hers. She surrendered to the love she felt for David, knowing after he left she would have to deal with all the doubts that plagued her. Right now she just wanted to be cherished and cherish in return.

"Coach, can I have a word with you?" Andy asked after delivering part of the scenery for the play/talent show at the refuge.

"Yeah. What do you need?" David set the last section of the backdrop in place.

"I have something else I need to bring in. Can you help me?"

"Sure," David said although puzzled by what Andy had said.

He'd been outside and hadn't seen anything that needed two people. Only the small pieces were left.

When David approached the trailer, all he saw was a small round table, easily carried by one. "Something going on?"

Andy withdrew the last piece from the flatbed they'd used to bring some of the scenery over from the barn where they'd painted it. "I didn't want Joey to overhear us talking." He glanced toward the entrance, then continued, "A few days ago at school when we got out for break, I saw a couple of older teens talking with Joey. He wasn't too happy. In fact, one took hold of his arm, and he jerked free and hurried to his bus. He was scared. Joey's never scared."

"Do you know the teens?"

"No, but they glared at Joey as the bus left. I think something bad is going on."

"You might very likely be right. Did you say anything to Joey about it?"

"No, we aren't exactly friends. I just thought you should know."

"If you see those guys again, see if you can find out their names. It might be nothing." But David thought Andy's instincts were dead on. One of those older boys could be Joey's supplier. "Can you describe any of them?"

"There were three. The one I think is the leader—he did all the talking—is tall, over six feet and muscular like he uses steroids or something. He wore a Mohawk and had several earrings, a nose ring. I used to see him pick up Joey from basketball practice sometimes." Andy thought for a moment. "His hair's brown. The others were blond and medium height. I don't remember much else."

"That's a start. I'll ask around." He'd talk with someone in Vice and see if he knew anyone who fit the description.

"Please don't say anything to Joey. We have a truce right

now, and he'd be mad if he knows I went to you. He saw me when he sat down on the bus. He knows I was watching him."

"This will stay between us, but if you see those guys again, let me know." David picked up the table and started for the entrance. Everything came back to drugs. He'd known when he decided to mentor Joey that he might be thrust into the middle of the drug scene again. Dread blanketed him as he paused on the stoop into the rec hall.

"Actually Joey's been pretty decent at school. Some don't know what to make of it."

"No bullying?"

"Well, he hasn't totally changed, but not nearly as much. In fact, last week he came to the defense of someone who isn't a friend."

"That's good." After Andy opened the door, David entered. "Are you ready to perform tonight?"

"I don't understand how Gabe and Terry talked me into singing. But they wouldn't take no for an answer."

"That sounds like your mother." David searched the large room and found Lisa over by the food tables, helping to set up the goodies for the party after the Christmas program.

He cared about her more than he should. He should walk away from her before he fell totally in love with her. He wouldn't be good for her. He carried around too much baggage—the conversation he'd just had with Andy proved that—and Lisa had her life on the right track. Although he hadn't known her as a drug addict, he'd seen enough of them while patrolling the streets of Dallas to see how much she had changed. That accomplishment awed him. But after the holidays, he needed to back off, let her get on with her life and find someone who'd take care of her. She deserved that much.

Chapter Twelve

Andy, Gabe and Terry came out onto the temporary stage in the rec hall to close the Christmas program. Lisa tensed. Andy had practiced for the past several weeks, and she could tell he was very nervous. He hadn't eaten a bite most of the day.

Andy rubbed his palms down his new black dress slacks while Gabe stepped forward to announce their song, their updated version of "The Twelve Days of Christmas." Behind them as the boys sang the first verse, one of the children from the cottage, dressed up as a flamingo in a tutu strutted across the stage. As each stanza was sung, someone illustrated the words.

She leaned close to David and whispered, "I volunteered to be the three chocolate bars, but the kids told me no adults were allowed on stage."

"Yeah, I was getting hungry watching Joey eat the three bars. I wonder how much he had to practice that particular skill."

She laughed. "Eating is a skill now?"

Hannah shifted in her chair toward Lisa. "Shh, you two. I'm trying to listen."

"Sorry." Color flooded Lisa's face. In her defense she was

nervous and needed to do something other than just sitting. Andy's tension had rubbed off on her throughout the day. On top of that, David had asked her to attend the midnight Christmas service at church. As his date. He'd made that very clear.

The song ended, and Andy came forward on stage. "We also have a surprise song we've been rehearsing for y'all. Just in case you've forgotten the reason we are here celebrating." Then he took a step back into line with Gabe and Terry.

Gabe gave a signal to someone off to the side and the music started for "O Holy Night." By the time the song was over, tears ran down Lisa's cheeks. She hadn't realized how beautiful her son's voice was until he did a solo in the middle. David reached over and took her hand. Her gaze slid to his, and in the depth of his eyes she saw that the words affected him as though he finally got it. He understood what the Christmas season was all about.

Thank you, Lord.

When the three boys finished "O Holy Night," the audience sat for a few seconds in complete silence, then suddenly the room exploded with applause and shouts of "bravo." David rose, clapping louder than anyone. Lisa's heart expanded at the sight of her son beaming at the people who filled the hall.

Andy flew off the stage and planted himself in front of her and David. "What y'all think?"

"I—I…" She didn't have the appropriate words to express how moved she'd been.

Andy's forehead crinkled.

"It was fantastic!" David patted him on the shoulder. "I didn't know you could sing so well."

"Neither did I. Gabe's the singer, but he talked me into doing this with him and Terry. He wanted to surprise his mom."

"Well, you surprised me." Lisa tapped her chest. "I'm rarely without words, but as you can see, I was. David put it nicely."

She spied Joey off to the side, watching them. She motioned him over. Reluctantly he prodded toward them, his expression wary.

"Joey, I was envious of you. I almost leaped on that stage and snatched a chocolate bar from you."

He looked away, mumbling something.

She was almost afraid to ask, "What?" but she did, wanting to include the young teen.

"They were okay." He glanced at her. "At least I wasn't the flamingo in a tutu. I drew the line at that."

Andy laughed. "I think we asked every guy involved in the program to do it. We thought it would be funny if a boy was dressed up in that outfit, but we couldn't get one to agree. If it will make you feel better, you were the last one we asked."

Again Joey mumbled something under his breath, but Lisa didn't get any sense of hostility coming from the teen—only bafflement at all that was happening.

"I see Mitch. Gotta go." Joey shuffled away.

"It's okay if I ride to the midnight service with the other kids on the bus?" Andy asked, pulling his attention away from Joey.

"I figure you would. I have a ride with David. We'll be sitting with Kelli and her children if you want to join us."

Andy studied David for a few seconds. "I kinda told Gabe and Terry I would sit with them."

"That's okay. I'll see you at the birthday party after the service."

"Whose birthday party?" David asked after Andy left, making his way toward the refreshment table.

"Jesus. By the time the service is over, it will be Christmas. We always have a cake and punch before we go home."

"Oh, I should have figured as much. This is all new for me." He swept his arm to indicate the room full of people celebrating Christmas. "I usually worked the holiday because I didn't have a family. It gave the guys who did the day off to be with theirs."

"Maybe this is your time to enjoy the holidays with family and friends. It sounds like too many years where you didn't."

"Ever since I became a patrolman. Kelli wasn't too happy, but she had her children and husband to console her."

"Where is Kelli? I thought she was coming with her children."

"Abbey threw a fit. Didn't want to come tonight, so Kelli stayed home to be with her children. She works long hours and I suspect she feels guilty."

"Yeah, guilt can make people do things they don't want to or shouldn't."

"It can rule a person's life."

The adamant way he said that sentence underscored how much guilt ate at David. "I have firsthand experience about it. Beating yourself up over a regret, trying to ignore it as though it doesn't exist or playing the blame game won't take the guilt away. I tried each one of those."

He pulled her to the side away from the crowd. "What do you do?" An intensity vibrated off David.

"Forgive yourself, then move on. Don't look back. The past can't be changed. The present and even the future is what's important." She was learning that, too. What David was going through only emphasized that. It wasn't always easy to look forward, but she was making strides in that direction.

David sighed. "I don't know if I can do it. It's not like I haven't tried."

"Maybe you need help."

"From you?"

"No, from someone with more power than me."

"Hey, you two, what are you doing off by yourselves,"

Hannah said as she approached them in the corner by the stage. She glanced at David, then Lisa. "Did I interrupt something?"

"No, we were just talking. No big deal." But the tension in his body conveyed the opposite. "Y'all had a nice turnout."

"This seems to get bigger and bigger each year. Before long we'll need to move to the high school auditorium." Hannah faced the hall full of people.

"Well, you've got connections since Peter is the principal." Lisa thought of the present she had for David. More and more she knew it was what he needed to help him move on.

"C'mon and join in the fun, you two. And please eat some of the ton of dishes we have. I don't have enough storage places for the leftovers."

The rest of the evening at the rec hall sped by with shared laughter, good food and friends. David stayed by Lisa's side, even put his arm around her shoulder once, pulling her close to him.

When it was time to head to the church, she grabbed her oversized purse while David helped her with her warm coat. "We need to make a mad dash for your car. The wind is from the north and it's cold out there."

"We might have a white Christmas after all. I know the kids want one."

The last Christmas it snowed she'd been beat up and left for dead in an alley by her ex-boyfriend. The memory of snow and Christmas wasn't a warm one for her. "It's not all it's cracked up to be. The children may be disappointed, but there'll probably be snow for them sometime this winter."

"I'm sorry I brought it up. I forgot what you told me about four years ago at this time. I find life doesn't work out like in one of those holiday movies you see on TV."

"Where everything works out perfectly while it begins to snow? I agree."

"I believe my cynical attitude is rubbing off more and more on you."

"Has my Pollyanna outlook had an effect on you?" Lisa stopped at the entrance into the hall.

David cocked his head and thought a moment, as though he were mentally reviewing his attitude. Surprise flicked into his gaze. "Actually, it has."

Once outside, the bite of the wind pierced through her overcoat. Shivering, she jogged next to David who opened his passenger's door for her. After he slipped behind the steering wheel, he immediately turned on the car.

"It will take a while to warm up," David said while Lisa rubbed her hands together.

"I lost my gloves a few weeks ago. I've been so busy with the holidays I haven't had time to get a pair." She didn't have much money, so cheap was all she could afford.

"That's a perfect opening to this." Switching on the interior light, David reached into the back seat and brought a wrapped gift to the front, laying it in her lap. "Merry Christmas."

"You shouldn't have," she whispered, stunned by the gesture. She couldn't remember a gift at Christmas from a man—one she was interested in. No, it was more than that. One she trusted. One she loved. The feelings stunned her with their power.

"Lisa, you okay?"

She gave him a smile. "Yes." *Very all right*. She tore into the paper.

"I wrapped it myself."

"Yes, I can tell." She lifted the top off the oblong box.

"I know there's too much tape and I need to work on making the paper even—"

"David, I love this." Lisa pulled out first a set of black leather gloves, fur lined, followed by a black cashmere scarf and matching hat. She brought the scarf to her face and relished its softness against her cold skin. "Thank you. This will keep me warm." She wound it around her neck, then donned the hat and gloves. "What do you think?"

The softness in his expression matched the feel of the cashmere. "Perfect. I wanted to get you something you could use, and I noticed you didn't have a hat or gloves. The scarf I threw in extra."

She plopped her big purse on her lap and dug into it. "I didn't want you to see this until I could give it to you privately."

He took it from her grasp and looked up at her. "You shouldn't have."

"I could say the same to you."

"I thought you only bought gifts for Andy and the needy children."

"I made an exception this Christmas."

He gingerly peeled back the red-and-silver paper and revealed a black Bible with his name engraved on the front in gold letters. His mouth fell open.

"If you don't want it—"

"No, I don't have one and have been thinking about getting one."

"I noticed in the adult class on Sunday you've been asking some questions. I think this will help you answer some of them." He was searching what the Lord wanted from His children, what was expected of him if he was a Christian.

He leaned over, tugged her across the console and kissed her. "I'm gonna miss you tomorrow."

He would spend the day with his sister and her family, while she and Andy went over to Hannah's as they had for the past few years. "I should be home by seven tomorrow night. Call me and tell me how your day went."

He caressed her hair behind her ear. "Can I stop by and tell you in person?"

"I'll have the hot chocolate ready. Who knows? I might even bake some ginger snaps."

He chuckled and gave her a quick kiss, then straightened and threw the car into reverse. "Are you sure you won't be home earlier than seven?"

"Probably not. It's hard to drag Andy away from his best friends."

"I've got a gift for Andy, too, but I'll wait and give it to him tomorrow night." He threw her a look. "I'm actually looking forward to the day. A first in a long time."

Lisa scanned the game room that held several groups of mothers and their young children but was otherwise empty. Mitch was seeing to the children and any needs that might arise. After two weeks with the kids off for winter break and spending a great deal of time at The Ultimate Pizzeria, it was almost deserted now that school was back in session.

Lisa turned into the main dining room. Having been through this before, she wasn't concerned about the lack of customers. These few hours between lunch and dinner were a good time to do some of her reports for Noah or ordering because this evening would most likely be crowded even on a school night.

Like her life lately—crowded with activities. She looked forward to some downtime now that the holidays had passed. But when she thought back over the past month with David, she couldn't help but smile. A special memory was Christmas night when he'd stopped by after being at his sister's all day. After Andy retired for the night, thrilled by his gift of a ticket to see the pro basketball team in Oklahoma City, David and she had sat in her living room with the lights dim, listening to for one last time Christmas music and talking quietly while sipping hot chocolate. She'd discovered David's favorite color was green, favorite series of books Winston Churchill's about World War II and favorite ice cream plain-old vanilla.

She weaved her way through the maze of tables toward her office in the back behind the counter, greeting a few stragglers enjoying a very late lunch. Out of the corner of her eye a movement caught her attention. She peered over her right shoulder to see David coming into the restaurant, making a beeline for her.

"What are you doing here?" she asked, pausing near the drink fountain.

"Stopping by to say hi to a friend. I saw your car out front and decided I needed to finally grab something to eat."

"Working through lunch again?"

"Yep. We got a hot tip on the robbery gang, and I just got through booking one of the suspects. It won't be long before the others are caught. I feel like celebrating tonight. Want to join me for dinner?"

"Here?"

David shook his head. "A fancy restaurant. It's about time I took you some place other than here."

She leaned close. "Shh. Don't let Noah hear you say that."

"He's here?"

"No, but you never know when he'll pop in."

"Roman told me about this little inn outside of town with a great restaurant, so I think he'll be okay. Wanna come with me?" he whispered into her ear.

A shiver zipped down her length from the warm caress of his breath and the minty scent of his toothpaste peppering the air. "You and Roman are becoming quite good friends," she finally said and took a step back to give her breathing room. His close proximity erased everything but him from her mind.

"When I'm not around, he's taking Joey under his wing at the refuge. At least when he's not fussing over Cathy."

"Yeah, I hate she hasn't been feeling well."

"So does Roman." David's cell on his belt buzzed. He withdrew it and flipped it open, saying, "I'd better get this. Be just a sec." David stepped a few feet away, turning from her, and spoke low into the phone.

She thought she heard him murmur, "I can't talk. I'll call you back."

When he was finished, he spun back toward her, a frown slashing his eyebrows. "I've got to go. Something's come up. Sorry. I'll call you later about tonight."

Before she could say anything, he was striding across the restaurant toward the exit. *Something has happened.* The rigidity to his gait told her anger festered below the surface. She wondered if it had anything to do with the robbery case. She slowly continued her trek to her office to work on the end-of-the-year report, but she couldn't forget the pale tinge that colored his face as he looked back at her after hanging up.

Please, Lord, keep him safe. I'm falling for him—hard.

In his car as he started the engine, David returned the earlier call. "Andy, where are you at school?" It had just let out, and Andy should have been on the bus on his way home.

"First, you didn't say anything to Mom, did you?"

"No, I'm heading toward the school now. Where are you exactly?" David asked in his calmest voice while his gut tightened at the fear he heard in the boy's voice.

"The three teens have dragged Joey across the street. They're heading for the alley running behind the houses. You've got to come. I can tell Joey is scared, and the guys are angry with him. You've got to help him."

"Now listen closely. Under no circumstances do I want you to do anything. Get out of there. I'll check out the alley and take care of everything. Understand?"

"Hurry, Coach." A pause then Andy said in a frantic voice, "Oh, no. They're beating him up."

"Andy—"

Lisa's son's phone clicked off. Fear played havoc with David's mind, images of past situations gone bad flashing across his thoughts in chilling waves. He put a call into the station for backup, then started to punch in Lisa's number, but instead tossed his cell on the seat and floored his Jeep. He was only a few minutes out and like Andy he wanted to protect her.

Chapter Thirteen

David slammed on his brakes, quickly leaping from his car in front of the series of homes across the street from the middle school that Andy had talked about. David jogged between the houses in order to get to the alley in the back. His heart pumped his blood at a dizzying speed through his body. His adrenaline escalated to full alert. He went for his gun. Again flashes of the past darted in and out of his mind. He saw the face of the dead thirteen-year-old; he shook his head, determined to focus on the situation at hand.

The sounds of fists hitting flesh quickened his step in the direction of the noise. Fear—for Andy, for Joey—taunted his ability to end this peaceably without anyone seriously getting hurt.

When he stepped out into the alley a few yards from the fight, gun in hand, he shut down his emotions in order to do what he had to. One adolescent had Andy pinned against him, while the other pounded at him, striking his body, clipping his jaw. A third teen with a knife hovered over Joey on the ground. His still form heightened the urgency.

"Police. Drop the knife," David shouted in his toughest voice.

The one holding Andy released him and fled down the alley with his cohort quickly escaping, too. Andy crumbled to the earth.

"Drop the knife now."

The last adolescent glared at David, the steel blade inches from Joey's face. David could see in his eyes the war raging over finishing what he started or doing what he was ordered. He glanced around him.

"Don't do it." David moved closer, his weapon trained on the lone teenager standing now over Joey. "Andy, you okay?"

"Yes, but Joey's hurt bad," the boy mumbled as though it were difficult to talk.

The sounds of footsteps approaching from both ends of the alley alerted David his backup had arrived. The assailant peered toward his right, then left. Resignation dawned in his eyes. He opened his hand and the knife slipped to the ground, barely missing Joey's arm.

David covered the space between him and the teen and forced him down with his legs spread while he handcuffed him. At that moment his reinforcements closed in. "Did you get the other two fleeing the scene?"

"Yeah, they're in the squad car with my partner," one patrol officer said, jerking the third teen to his feet.

David knelt by Joey. When he noticed the rise and fall of Joey's chest, relief shuddered through him.

"Is Joey dead?" Andy asked in a quavering voice as he slowly pushed himself to his feet and hobbled toward them.

"No. This looks bad, but he'll be okay," David said that more to reassure himself than from any knowledge he was right. He looked toward his backup. "Call for an ambulance."

"Already have," one officer said, taking possession of the knife by Joey. "We'll take this one in." He jerked his head toward the assailant, and he and his partner left with the third teen held between them.

"I'll stay until the ambulance arrives," the first patrolman on the scene said, checking out the alley.

David's gaze finally fell on Andy on the other side of Joey. Andy's face looked worse than it had that time outside the gym in November. He would have to have stitches. That thought brought a frown to his mouth. "You were supposed to remain hidden, wait for me." He inwardly winced at the hard edge to his words, but if he'd been delayed a couple of more minutes, Andy very likely would have been in the same condition as Joey.

"I couldn't. They kept hitting his head into the ground. Then that big one pulled a knife. He was gonna cut Joey. I couldn't let him kill Joey. I knew you were coming. I was just trying to buy some time."

"Yeah, well, you could have gotten yourself killed." The sound of the ambulance approaching blared through the cold air. "I've got to call your mom."

"No!"

"You can't keep this from her. You should see your face. My cell is in my Jeep. Let me have yours."

Reluctantly Andy dug into his pocket and pulled it out. He handed it to David as the ambulance came to a halt near them.

David stood and allowed the EMTs to put Joey on the gurney. "He hasn't regained consciousness. His head was pounded into the ground."

"Someone did a number on him," one of the paramedics said, staring at Andy.

"Yeah, we took them into custody. I'll be following you to the hospital." David's hand settled on Andy's shoulder. "This one needs to be checked out, too, so I'll take him."

After the ambulance pulled away, David started toward his

Jeep with Andy next to him. David flipped open the boy's cell and punched in Lisa's work number. When she answered the phone, he saw an anguished expression descend over Andy's features.

"Lisa, I'm at the middle school. I need you to meet me at the hospital. Andy's been hurt—" he heard Lisa gasp and hurriedly went on "—but he's okay. He'll need some stitches, though." He barely caught his breath between sentences, his words rushing out.

"What happened?"

"A fight. It would be faster to meet me at the emergency room than to come here."

She clicked off without saying anything else. Through the connection he could practically feel her confusion, anger and worry.

"She's gonna be so mad," Andy muttered as he slid into the front seat.

Yeah, at me. Although Andy wouldn't tell him where he was without David's promise not to tell his mother what was going on with Joey, he'd agreed Lisa didn't need to know because she would have wanted to come with him to the school. Her presence would have complicated the situation. But she might not see it that way.

Lisa came out of the exam room in the E.R. where Andy was being sewn up and strode up to David, fury carving the planes of her face with a hard edge. "I was standing right there with you when Andy called you for help. What were you thinking not telling me about what was going on?"

"I needed to move fast and without you tagging along." When she'd first come into the emergency room, her silence and avoidance of him after she'd listened to the explanation of what had happened should have warned him of her reaction. But its intensity still took him by surprise.

She started to say something else, shook her head and snapped her mouth closed. Clamping her lips together, she narrowed her gaze on his face and finally muttered, "That's not a good answer. I trusted you."

"That's the only answer I have. I didn't need you in danger, too. You were safer at the restaurant." That was his job, to keep others safe, not to knowingly put someone in danger. "If you really trust me, then you'll trust that I did what I thought was best."

She poked him in the chest. "You obviously don't know me very well after all the time we've spent together. My place is by my child's side no matter what. I don't need protection and both you and Andy better get that through your thick heads." Throwing up her hands, she backed away from him. "A knife! He could have been killed."

A nerve jerked in his jaw line. "And what would you have done? You would have hampered what I had to do." He'd seen it before where a loved one would rush in and put the person they wanted to save in peril by their actions.

"Clearly I was reading more into our relat—friendship than there was. If you can't trust me to do what is best, then I think we need to go our separate ways. I fought too hard to get Andy back to have you make decisions about him without including me." She spun on her heel and marched back into the examination room.

He began to go after her but halted his movement in mid-stride. This was for the best. His need to protect was one of the reasons he'd become a police officer. He couldn't change for her, and it had nothing to do with trust. Or did it? Long ago he'd become a miser when it came to his trust. He'd given up trusting others, himself and the Lord, and no relationship could move forward without that trust.

His shoulders sagged forward as he sat again, waiting to hear from Jacob concerning Joey's injuries. David had called him to tell him about Joey. The doctor had arrived twenty minutes later and disappeared into the examination room, promising to tell him what was going on.

Restless, David surged to his feet and paced the length of the hallway, hoping the patrol officer he'd sent to find Mitch would get here soon with Joey's brother. The strong urge to seek advice swamped David, but who could he talk to? The person who had listened to him lately didn't want to see him anymore.

He headed for the vending machines just outside the E.R. Depositing some coins, he punched the button for coffee but winced when he took a sip. Bitterness tainted his mouth. He threw the mostly full cup away and turned. His gaze swept the long hallway. He glimpsed the chapel sign.

Without considering his actions, he trudged toward the place. Thankfully Joey had regained consciousness in the ambulance. While the paramedics had wheeled him into the hospital, the teen had looked so defenseless and small. Blood covered his battered face and clothes. When he and Joey had locked gazes, all David had seen was vulnerability in the boy's expression.

In the chapel, relieved no one else was there, David sat in a chair near the front of the room. The dim lighting soothed his tattered nerves. Back at the alley there had been a moment when he'd hesitated pulling his gun, the kid he'd killed in Dallas dominating his thoughts for a few possibly crucial seconds. He couldn't run from the truth any longer. He needed to find another profession. He wanted so badly to discuss this with Lisa, but after what happened, she'd slam the door in his face.

What do I do, Lord? Where do I go from here?

Nothing.

He sat another fifteen minutes, leaving his mind open to an answer from God, but silence greeted him. Disappointment weighed him down as he trudged toward the E.R.

* * *

At the apartment Lisa paced the living room, having brought her son home half an hour ago, hurting, but okay. She'd been too angry to say much to him, but it was time to get a few things straight with Andy.

She started toward his bedroom when his door flew open and he emerged, changed into a clean pair of jeans and a sweatshirt. "We need to talk."

"Yeah, I know, but I want you to take me back to see Joey at the hospital."

"Why? That child has only brought you bad news."

"Because he needs a friend and he'll be in pain." Andy set his jaw as though gritting his teeth. "Mom, Joey could have died today. I have things to say to him, should have weeks ago."

"You could have died today! Has that not gotten through to you?"

"Yeah, when those guys were hitting me." He touched his bruised face. "Fists hurt."

She jammed her balled hands on her hips. "Why didn't you want David to tell me what was happening when you called him?"

"Because you would have tried to stop me from following Joey and those guys."

"And David didn't?"

"Well, yeah, but I couldn't very well let them kill Joey."

"There were three of them and just you. What made you think you could do anything?"

Andy looked her in the eye. "God. He was with me."

Her mouth dropped open. She didn't know what to say to that. Finally she settled on her original question. "Why didn't you want me to know?"

"Because I don't want you involved in any way with

anything to do with drugs. They had them and were showing Joey. They kept yelling about some drugs he had of theirs. He either had to give them back or pay him. I think they were the ones the police took from Joey."

Something in her deflated at the Andy's explanation. "You don't have to protect me, Andy. I'm not gonna take drugs again. At the women's shelter I counsel some of them about drugs. There is no temptation anymore. *None*. I see how messed up some of the ladies' lives are, and I don't ever want to go back to that. You don't have to be the grown-up anymore." She closed the distance between them and drew him against her. "Hon, I want you to be a kid. Enjoy your childhood. There'll be time later for you to be an adult. I'm doing just fine."

Andy leaned back, tears in his eyes. "Don't be mad at David. I'm the one you should blame. Promise me you'll forgive him."

She remembered telling David he needed to forgive himself in order to move on in his life. How could she not forgive him? She smoothed her son's hair from his face. "Don't you worry about a thing."

"Will you take me to the hospital to see Joey?"

"Why don't you wait until he goes home tomorrow? I'll take you out to the refuge then." She was afraid David would be there and she didn't want to see him until she cooled down—thought things through.

"Mom, I need to make sure he's all right. Please."

She couldn't deny her son's request. She nodded.

"This was all my fault," Mitch said, standing at the end of Joey's hospital bed.

"Why do you say that?" David pulled the blinds over the window now that it was night.

Joey's brother clenched the railing on the bed. "Those guys were my friends once. Joey got to know them because of me."

"Did you know what was going on? What your friends were into?"

"Yeah. That's why we were no longer friends. I'd seen what had happened to some of my older buddies. I didn't want that for me or Joey."

"Did you know they had approached Joey about selling drugs at the middle school?"

"No, but then I've been very busy with finishing school and working to support us. I wasn't around as much as I should have been."

David glanced at Joey, lying in the bed. He'd been slipping in and out of sleep for the past few hours. "You aren't Joey's father. You're his brother. And blaming yourself won't change what happened. Don't go down that road. I know personally no good comes from it."

"How can I not?" Mitch gestured toward his brother. "Look at him. You can hardly recognize him because of the beating."

"I'll tell you why you shouldn't." David drew in a fortifying breath, only once before telling someone what he'd gone through with the shooting. "While I worked in Dallas a couple of years ago, I killed a teen in the line of duty. He was thirteen years old. Had his whole life before him, and he was mixed up in drugs because of his older brother. For the past two years my life has been on hold because of that shooting. I blamed myself for the kid's death. Only lately have I started to realize I didn't have a choice. Don't get me wrong. I'll always regret what happened that day, but blaming myself wouldn't change it or the fact the kid's older brother had him there as a lookout and had placed a gun in his hand. A good friend told me I had to forgive myself and look toward the future, not back at the past. And she's right."

Mitch hung his head, staring at the end of the bed. "I want my brother back, but I think he's in the best place for him right now."

"Yeah, I have to agree with you on that although I doubt Joey does."

"Hopefully one day he will." Mitch released his tight grip on the railing.

"You should go get something to eat. I'll be here if he wakes up again."

As Mitch left the room, David checked his watch and saw the date. Today was the second anniversary of the shooting, and he hadn't realized it. He knew then that he'd meant what he'd told Mitch about blaming himself for something he couldn't avoid—out of his control. He wasn't going back to that man who pushed everyone who cared about him away to cover up his wounds.

But, Lord, I still don't know what to do with that future You say I should focus on.

The swishing sound of the door opening drew his attention. Peter and Roman entered the room.

"How's he doing?" Roman asked, coming to the other side of the bed.

"He's gonna be hurting for a while, but he'll heal physically."

Peter frowned. "Two of those teens went to my school. The other had dropped out last year. I hope this incident will finally wake up the board of education. I've been pushing for them to hire a drug counselor for the school district. This problem isn't going to go away."

"Sadly, I agree." David kneaded the tight cords of his neck.

Joey shifted, a moan escaping his lips. His eyes fluttered open, then closed for a moment. "Thirsty."

David moved to the pitcher and poured a cup of water. "Here you go."

Joey reached for the drink, his hand shaking. David steadied the child's hold and helped him take a couple of sips.

"We just wanted to stop by and see how you were doing. Everyone at the refuge is praying for you and hopes you'll be home soon." Roman withdrew a snapshot from his front shirt pocket and gave it to the boy. "I thought I'd bring a picture of Bolt for you. He misses you already."

"He does?" Joey stared at the photo of the potbellied pig in his pen.

"Yeah, he's moping around. Hasn't tried once today to get out of his pen. Right before Peter and I came, I had the door to his stall wide open and Bolt just stood there staring at me as if he was waiting for you to come."

Joey tried to laugh but winced.

Peter stepped up beside Roman. "Jacob tells me we can pick you up tomorrow afternoon. They want to run a few more tests in the morning, but then you'll be free to come home."

Joey blinked rapidly when Peter said the word home.

"And the kids in your cottage signed this card for you." Peter laid it on Joey's lap. "We'll see you tomorrow."

After Peter and Roman left, Joey opened the card, confusion entering his eyes. "They care," he murmured through swollen lips.

"Yeah, a lot of people care about you."

Joey reached toward the beside table to put the card next to the photo of Bolt, his movements slow, pain glazing his eyes.

"Hey, I can do that for you." David plucked the card from Joey's grip and placed it upright so he could see the front of it, then David propped Bolt's picture up against the pitcher.

"Thanks," Joey mumbled and closed his eyes.

Silence fell between them, and David thought Joey had

drifted off to sleep again, but when the door opened, the kid's eyes eased open. David glanced toward the entrance. Andy hobbled into the room with Lisa following him.

Andy planted himself next to the bed. "You look like you've been in a fight and lost."

"You didn't do too good yourself." Joey cocked a grin that instantly disappeared.

David's gaze snared Lisa's. Nothing in her eyes indicated she regretted her earlier anger. "How are you doing?" David asked Andy, wanting to ask Lisa the same question.

"I'll recover. It may take a little longer than last time."

"I'm sorry about that," Joey mumbled, averting his gaze to the end of the bed. "Thanks for trying to help me."

"No big deal." Andy shifted his weight to the other foot, then back.

Joey looked back at him. "Yes, it was. To me. I don't think anyone's ever done something like that for me."

"We're friends. Friends help each other."

Joey tried to say something but ended up swallowing hard several times. "I'm also sorry about putting those pills into your drink. I wanted you to get into trouble. You always thought you were better than me. That you would never stoop to my level and have anything to do with drugs."

Andy straightened, sliding his gaze to Lisa, then back to Joey. "I won't. But I'm not better than you—just different." He grinned. "And you play a mean game of basketball."

"Maybe next year I'll get back on the team."

"I hope. We could use you. Anyway, I just needed to make sure you were okay," Andy said as his mom came up behind him and laid her hand on his shoulder.

"We both wanted to make sure you were all right." Lisa avoided eye contact with David, keeping her attention totally on Joey.

In that moment David realized that she might never talk to him again. He also realized Lisa Morgan was the best thing that had ever happened to him and he couldn't let her walk out of his life without a fight.

Lisa squeezed her son's shoulder. "We don't want to stay long, but we'll check on you at the refuge."

Andy started to turn away when Joey asked, "Why did you do it?"

Andy stopped and peered back at him. "Because it was the right thing to do. I couldn't stand by and watch them seriously hurt you or worse."

"But the things I did to you."

"That's the past. Over. Done."

One corner of his swollen lips lifted. "Thanks."

"You're welcome. See you tomorrow."

As Lisa and Andy made their way toward the door, David rounded the end of the bed. "Wait, Lisa. Can I speak with you?"

She glanced over her shoulder. "Not tonight. It's been a long day." Her words, spoken in a flat tone, emphasized their earlier encounter outside the exam room.

David watched her walk out of his life. *Lord, I could use Your help here.*

"What are you doing here?" Lisa asked as she opened her front door wider to allow Hannah into the apartment.

"Before I pick up Joey, I thought I would stop by and see how Andy is doing."

"He's not here. He wanted to go to school this morning. He wanted to make a statement about drugs not winning."

"Then I guess he's okay."

"I wouldn't say that, but he wouldn't stay home no matter how much I tried to get him to."

Hannah hiked her purse onto her shoulder. "How are you holding up?"

"Not as good as Andy. He seems to be shaking off this whole incident. I can't. I'm so angry with David. I…"

"He did what he thought was best. He's trained to handle situations like that. You aren't. Ideally, Andy wouldn't have been hurt at all if he hadn't chosen to try and break them up before they did more harm to Joey."

"So I should be mad at Andy?"

"No, but let go of that anger. It doesn't do any good or at the very least direct it at those teens being held." Hannah flipped her hair behind her shoulders. "What's the real reason you are so mad at David?"

"Real reason? That's it."

"This past month I've seen you with him, and it's clear to anyone who knows you well, you were falling in love with him."

"No, I don't…" Lisa's denial sputtered to an end. "Okay, I was, but it would never have worked between us. Andy doesn't care for cops." The incident with Andy brought her back to reality. *How can a police officer really love a recovering addict?*

"Well, then David is the exception, and I think you know that."

"You know about my past. I'm damaged goods."

"And David knows about your past and still hangs around. In fact, he went out of his way to make sure he was a part of your life—and for that matter, Andy's." Hannah took her hands. "All I'm asking you is to talk to him. Don't let it end on anger. You have a lot to offer a man. You have come so far in the years I've known you. I'm so proud of your accomplishments." Her friend hugged her, then turned toward the door. "I'd better get going. Joey's already called once today. He wants to get out of the hospital."

After Hannah left, Lisa sank down on the couch and stared

at a spot across the room. In her mind she saw again David's crestfallen expression as she'd told him she didn't want to talk to him last night. She closed her eyes, but still the picture haunted her. They did need to talk. She just needed to think about how to do it and what to say.

In the meantime, she had to be at work. Pushing to her feet, she hurried into her bedroom to finish getting ready. Five minutes later she gathered up her purse and took out her car keys before heading toward the door. Outside on the second floor landing, after locking up, she started for the stairs.

At the bottom stood David, his hand on the railing. Their gazes connected.

Before she could say or do anything, he mounted the steps, saying, "I think we should talk. Or at least I talk and you listen."

"Oh, and I don't have a say in it?"

"After I have my say, I'll leave if you want me to."

"I have to be at work."

"Call your boss and tell her you're gonna be a little late."

Lisa backed up until she could go no farther. "Okay, what do you have to say?"

He gestured toward her apartment. "Let's go inside. *Please*."

She unlocked her door and entered, awareness shivering down her spine. As she slowly rotated toward David, the urge to throw herself into his arms flooded her. She held her ground. Andy could have been killed yesterday. She and David were too different. She'd known that from the beginning.

"I didn't want Andy to do what he did. I asked him to stay put and I'd be there to take care of the situation. Knowing how it turned out, I still wouldn't have said anything to you, Lisa." When she opened her mouth to stop him, he held up his hand. "Please, let me explain. You knowing wouldn't have changed the outcome, but it could have put you in harm's way or even

Andy more than he already was. Would you have stayed by the Jeep and waited for me to investigate? Be honest with yourself."

Would she have? No, she would have charged after David. She shook her head.

"Do you see my dilemma? I couldn't do the job the way I needed to if I was worrying about you and Andy. I couldn't take that risk, especially with children's lives possibly at stake. I didn't want something to happen like in Dallas." He took several steps closer. "I want you and Andy in my life. Don't throw away what I think you and I have together."

The past few months paraded across her mind—David trying patiently to reach her son, his explanation about the shooting, her confession, the laughter they had shared, the pain, too. She peered deep into his eyes and saw something in them she'd never seen in another man's—at least not toward her. It was the same look Jacob had for Hannah.

Was she reading him correctly? "What do you think you and I have?"

"You gonna make me say it, aren't you?"

She nodded. "I want no misunderstandings between us."

"I love you, Lisa. You have broken down every barrier I put in your way. You wouldn't give up on me. I want a forever with you. Will you marry me?"

She did what she'd been wanting to do ever since he walked into her apartment. She threw her arms around him and kissed him, pouring all her love into it.

When he parted, leaning back to stare down at her, he cupped her face. "Is that a yes to a forever?"

"I thought you were a top-notch detective. Figure it out."

Epilogue

"Here I was thinking we should elope. Now I'm glad we didn't. You're beautiful." David caged Lisa against him right outside the double doors into the reception hall of their church as their guests waited for their entrance.

His eyes shone with all the love she'd come to expect from him over the months. Now a year from the date they'd met, they had become husband and wife. "I have to admit eloping began to sound good when Hannah, Whitney and Kelli started planning this wedding."

"You ready to go in and face everyone?"

She laughed. "You make it sound like torture."

"I'd rather skip the reception and head right for the honeymoon, but I'm afraid if we did, we'd better not come back here."

"My friends aren't that bad. Look what your buddies on the police force did."

"Yeah, I was kinda surprised by the motorcade because I resigned a few months ago."

"I guess once a police officer, always one." She snuggled against him and stood on her tiptoes to plant a kiss on his mouth.

"But I for one am glad you're working for the school as their drug counselor. You're perfect for the job, but then I'm biased."

David wound his arms around Lisa. "No regrets, Mrs. Russell?"

"None, Mr. Russell. I love you," she murmured right before David gave her a kiss that rocked her to her core.

"Hey, you two, you can do that later. You've got some hungry guests waiting for you to make your grand entrance." Roman threw the doors wide open to reveal the large room filled with friends and family.

Everyone she cared about stood before her. Andy in front with Joey, his brother not far from him. Hannah and Jacob, the two who had saved her. Whitney and Kelli, whom she still got together with on Saturdays.

David faced the wall of people, taking her hand. "An hour. Then we're out of here. We have a honeymoon to start."

* * * * *

Dear Reader,

When I decided to tell Lisa's story (she first appeared in *Heart of the Family*), I knew I had to deal with drugs because she had been an addict. It wasn't something I could gloss over or ignore. Having for many years worked as a teacher at a high school, I know how prevalent drugs are in the schools. It's not something that can be ignored.

If you think you know of a problem, there are some sites on the Internet that can help: National Institute on Drug Abuse at www.nida.nih.gov, Substance Abuse and Mental Health Service Administration at www.samhsa.gov and National Institute on Alcohol and Alcoholism at www.niaaa.nih.gov. Or you can contact the nearest Area Prevention Resource Center.

I love to hear from readers. You can contact me at: P.O. Box 2074, Tulsa 74101, or you can e-mail me at: margaretdaley@gmail.com. To learn more about my books, visit my Web site at www.margaretdaley.com.

Best wishes,

Margaret Daley

QUESTIONS FOR DISCUSSION

1. Lisa is a recovering drug addict. She credits her turnaround to God. Have you or a loved one ever faced an addiction? What helped to deal with it and overcome it?

2. David is a law officer who ended up killing someone in the line of duty. He thought he could cope with it but discovered he couldn't. His guilt consumed him. Has this happened to you? What did you do to get over the guilt? Have you succeeded?

3. Who is your favorite character? Why?

4. Andy tried to handle a problem by himself. He got in over his head. What should he have done when Joey started bullying him?

5. Andy wanted to protect his mother but ended up hurt when he tried. Lisa had a hard time getting him to understand he didn't need to protect her. What advice would you give Lisa in this situation?

6. At the beginning Lisa couldn't figure out what to do about Andy's changing. For the first time she was being shut out of his life. Has this happened to you? How did you deal with your frustration and feelings of impotence?

7. What is your favorite scene? Why?

8. One of my themes is forgiveness. David needed to forgive himself. He couldn't until Lisa showed him how. Is there

someone you need to forgive? What steps can you take to heal the rift?

9. Why is it important to forgive ourselves and others? What happens when we live in the past rather than looking forward to the future? Which do you focus on—past, present or future? Why?

10. The illegal sale of prescription drugs is a problem in our schools. What are some steps we can take to change that? What should be done with a young teen found selling drugs to his peers?

11. I called the program Joey was going through the Seven Steps to Healing. I based it on a real program that a place in Oklahoma is using to help young teens overcome addiction and anger. The program deals with the underlying reasons that people become addicted. Do you have similar programs in your area? What makes those programs successful?

12. I enjoy writing about flawed characters who fight to get their lives on track. Have you ever felt as if you were on a runaway train headed for a wreck? How did you get off that train?

*Here's a sneak peek at
"Merry Mayhem" by Margaret Daley,
one of the two riveting suspense stories in the
new collection CHRISTMAS PERIL,
available in December 2009 from
Love Inspired Suspense.*

"**R**un. Disappear… Don't trust anyone, especially the police."

Annie Coleman almost dropped the phone at her ex-boyfriend's words, but she couldn't. She had to keep it together for her daughter. Jayden played nearby, oblivious to the sheer terror Annie was feeling at hearing Bryan's gasped warning.

"Thought you could get away," a gruff voice she didn't recognize said between punches. "You haven't finished telling me what I need to know."

Annie panicked. What was going on? What was happening to Bryan on the other end? Confusion gripped her in a choke-hold, her chest tightening with each inhalation.

"I don't want—" Bryan's rattling gasp punctuated the brief silence "—any money. Just let me go. I'll forget everything."

"I'm not worried about you telling a soul." The menace in the assailant's tone underscored his deadly intent. "All I need to know is exactly where you hid it. If you tell me now, it will be a lot less painful."

"I can't—" Agony laced each word.

"What's that? A phone?" the man screamed.

The sounds of a struggle then a gunshot blasted her eardrum. Curses roared through the connection.

Fear paralyzed Annie in the middle of her kitchen. Was Bryan shot? Dead?

The voice on the phone returned. "Who's this? Who are you?"

The assailant's voice so clear on the phone panicked her. She slammed it down onto its cradle as though that action could sever the memories from her mind. But nothing would. Had she heard her daughter's father being killed? What information did Bryan have? Did that man know her name? Question after question bombarded her from all sides, but inertia held her still.

The ringing of the phone jarred her out of her trance. Her gaze zoomed in on the lighted panel on the receiver and saw the call was from Bryan's cell. The assailant had her home telephone number. He could discover where she lived. He knew what she'd heard.

"Mommy, what's wrong?"

Looking up at Jayden, Annie schooled her features into what she hoped was a calm expression while her stomach reeled. "You know, I've been thinking, honey, we need to take a vacation. It's time for us to have an adventure. Let's see how fast you can pack." Although she tried to make it sound like a game, her voice quavered, and Annie curled her trembling hands until her fingernails dug into her palms.

At the door, her daughter paused, cocking her head. "When will we be coming back?"

The question hung in the air, and Annie wondered if they'd ever be able to come back at all.

* * * * *

Follow Annie and Jayden as they flee to Christmas, Oklahoma, and hide from a killer—with a little help from a small-town police officer.

Look for CHRISTMAS PERIL by Margaret Daley and Debby Giusti, available December 2009 from Love Inspired Suspense.

REQUEST YOUR FREE BOOKS!

2 FREE INSPIRATIONAL NOVELS
PLUS 2
FREE
MYSTERY GIFTS

Love Inspired®

YES! Please send me 2 FREE Love Inspired® novels and my 2 FREE mystery gifts (gifts are worth about $10). After receiving them, if I don't wish to receive any more books, I can return the shipping statement marked "cancel". If I don't cancel, I will receive 4 brand-new novels every month and be billed just $4.24 per book in the U.S. or $4.74 per book in Canada. That's a savings of over 20% off the cover price. It's quite a bargain! Shipping and handling is just 50¢ per book.* I understand that accepting the 2 free books and gifts places me under no obligation to buy anything. I can always return a shipment and cancel at any time. Even if I never buy another book, the two free books and gifts are mine to keep forever.

113 IDN EYK2   313 IDN EYLE

Name	(PLEASE PRINT)

Address	Apt. #

City	State/Prov.	Zip/Postal Code

Signature (if under 18, a parent or guardian must sign)

Mail to Steeple Hill Reader Service:
IN U.S.A.: P.O. Box 1867, Buffalo, NY 14240-1867
IN CANADA: P.O. Box 609, Fort Erie, Ontario L2A 5X3
Not valid to current subscribers of Love Inspired books.

Want to try two free books from another series?
Call 1-800-873-8635 or visit www.morefreebooks.com

* Terms and prices subject to change without notice. Prices do not include applicable taxes. Sales tax applicable in N.Y. Canadian residents will be charged applicable provincial taxes and GST. Offer not valid in Quebec. This offer is limited to one order per household. All orders subject to approval. Credit or debit balances in a customer's account(s) may be offset by any other outstanding balance owed by or to the customer. Please allow 4 to 6 weeks for delivery. Offer available while quantities last.

Your Privacy: Steeple Hill Books is committed to protecting your privacy. Our Privacy Policy is available online at www.SteepleHill.com or upon request from the Reader Service. From time to time we make our lists of customers available to reputable third parties who may have a product or service of interest to you. If you would prefer we not share your name and address, please check here. ☐

LIREG09

Love Inspired®

HEARTWARMING INSPIRATIONAL ROMANCE

Get more of the heartwarming
inspirational romance stories that
you love and cherish, beginning
in July with SIX NEW titles,
available every month from
the Love Inspired® line.

Also look for our other
Love Inspired® genres, including:

Love Inspired® Suspense:
Enjoy four contemporary tales of intrigue
and romance every month.

Love Inspired® Historical:
Travel to a different time with two powerful
and engaging stories of romance, adventure
and faith every month.

*Available every month wherever books are sold,
including most bookstores, supermarkets,
drugstores and discount stores.*

www.SteepleHill.com

Steeple
Hill®

LIINCREASE2

TITLES AVAILABLE NEXT MONTH

Available November 24, 2009

THE SOLDIER'S HOLIDAY VOW by Jillian Hart
The Granger Family Ranch

Trapped in a mine shaft with a little girl, September Stevens prays for help. And then she is rescued by handsome army ranger Mark Hawkins. Can his Christmas vow offer her the love of a lifetime?

JINGLE BELL BABIES by Kathryn Springer
After the Storm

When Nurse Lori Martin hears that Jesse Logan is looking for a nanny for his triplet daughters, she can't help but offer her services. Lori soon discovers that all she wants for Christmas is a trio of giggling babies—and their handsome father.

LONE STAR BLESSINGS by Bonnie K. Winn
Rosewood, Texas

Widowed sheriff Tucker Grey needs an instruction manual to raise his preteen daughter. Until Sunday school teacher Kate Lambert steps in. But can she teach the lawman to open his heart?

HIS CHRISTMAS BRIDE by Dana Corbit
Wedding Bell Blessings

The only gift Dylan Warren used to want was Jenna Scott's love. But his former childhood best friend broke his heart. Now, their matchmaking mothers insist the two families celebrate the holiday together. Will wedding bells join the jingle bells?

JENNA'S COWBOY HERO by Brenda Minton

Jenna Cameron has got a plan: raising her twin boys, running her ranch—and *not* falling in love. But brand-new neighbor Adam McKenzie has some plans of his own, which include building a summer camp—and a permanent place in Jenna's heart.

A WEDDING IN WYOMING by Deb Kastner

Jenn Washington has found a way to take the focus off her nonexistent love life. Her make-believe boyfriend "Johnny" should do the trick, until real cowboy Johnny Barnes shows up at the front door!

LICNMBPA1109